DEAD MAN'S JOURNEY

The Civil War took everything from Alex Adamley. He was once the captain of the blockade runner the *Savannah Belle*. He'd been crippled; left penniless; his ship destroyed and his home and family gone. Yet his dead brother had left him some property in the distant West. Alex determined to go and see this property. He started walking ever westward . . . on a journey that would end in the toughest fight of his life. He was on a Dead Man's Journey.

FRANK RODERUS

DEAD MAN'S JOURNEY

Complete and Unabridged

LINFORD
Leicester

First published in Great Britain in 2007 by
Robert Hale Limited
London

First Linford Edition
published 2009
by arrangement with
Robert Hale Limited
London

British Library CIP Data

Roderus, Frank
    Dead man's journey.—Large print ed.—
Linford western library
    1. Western stories
    2. Large type books
    I. Title
    823.9'14 [F]

    ISBN 978–1–84782–548–3

Published by
F. A. Thorpe (Publishing)
Anstey, Leicestershire

Set by Words & Graphics Ltd.
Anstey, Leicestershire
Printed and bound in Great Britain by
T. J. International Ltd., Padstow, Cornwall

This book is printed on acid-free paper

1

I

Steady now, steady on. The thoughts were strong, but he remained silent, willing the men onward. The whaleboats were too far ahead for the crew to hear, even if he wanted them to. And he did not want them to. It would serve them ill if they knew his nervousness.

It was like this every time. Dark-dyed sails furled now that they'd closed on the inlet. Whaleboats forward to tow the *Belle* against the wind, sliding black and quiet through the night with the cargo so desperately needed.

God, he hated these moments. Most of the crew in the boats, while the remainder, save only himself and his helmsman, aloft, ready to loose the sails in case a shallow-draft Union sloop should find them. Ready to come about

1

and race for open water should they be discovered.

That was his rule. Stealth in, stealth out, and never offer the fight. More than three years, and he'd not lost a man yet. Nor a cargo. He did not intend for this to be the first time.

A quarter mile ahead lay the mouth of the creek that would swallow the *Belle* and make her invisible from the Union coasters. A quarter mile and closing. But slowly. So slowly. Captain Alex Adamley wished he could pick the craft up and make her surge forward to safe haven.

Ahead, the oars dipped and strained in practiced unison, drops of water sparkling like jewels in the faint starlight.

There was no moon. He never closed on the coast until moon and tide were as he needed. No more than a quarter moon and preferably not that. Tide incoming so as to help the oarsmen with the approach, then assist again after the swift and practiced task of offloading, ready for another run past the porous blockade and a passage to England, France, or the Bahamas.

He would have liked cloud, and the darker the better, but this night the sky was clear and the wind streamed gently from off the shore. That was to the good. In order to retreat, all they need do was let the sails out and whirl about, but only if they needed to abort the approach.

Now, however . . . now they sought the safety that lay inside the creek mouth those last few hundred yards ahead.

Adamley's hands tightened on the forward rail, and he strained to see.

The *Belle* was at her most vulnerable at this moment as they entered the lee caused by the trees ahead. The offshore breeze slackened, and now she was wholly dependent on the men in the whaleboats.

'Captain!' The voice came from one of the men in the rigging aloft.

Adamley stifled an impulse to growl

at the man for breaking his concentration. 'Aye?'

'I hear something, Captain. Splashing, like.'

'Where?'

'Aft, Captain. I hear a splashing sound aft.'

Adamley turned, eyes straining to cut through the night. He could make out the black on gray bulk of Hogthroat Island low against an invisible horizon. He could see —

Oh, God. Sweet Jesus!

White. Moving. Coming round the north tip of Hogthroat. A pale superstructure midship and flashes of white aft as it cleared the island. Black sails? No. No sails at all. The damnable thing was steam driven. That was what he saw in those white flashes. Foam raised by water streaming off the paddles as the squat and ugly craft wallowed gracelessly through the sea.

'Careful, men. Show no light,' he called in a voice far calmer than what he truly felt. 'If you've pale clothing, keep it behind something. We're close on the shore. Should be lost to his sight against the trees. Steady now. Hold steady.'

'There's another boat coming up from the south, Captain. Taking the inside passage he is, sir.'

It was too shallow down there, dammit. No man-o'-war could — oh, Lord. Steam driven paddles. A boat like that could navigate water that would ground any sailing vessel larger than a dinghy.

He, too, could see the gunboat approach from the south.

'Sir?'

The first boat had cleared the shoals at the tip of Hogthroat and turned now, straight at the *Belle*.

That boat stood directly in their only path for escape, the wind permitting no other. And the one coming north through the shallow passage between island and shore —

'All hands on deck,' Adamley ordered. 'All hands down, now. We'll not be needing sail this night.'

He gave thought to the guns. They had a pair of light chasers. That was all. And those had never been fired. Stealth was always the rule. Stealth and speed. And now . . .

'They may yet miss seeing us,' he called.

It was a foolish hope.

A ball of yellow flame blossomed from the prow of the gunboat to the south. The muzzle flash was startling, vividly bright in the night. That shot was quickly followed by a second.

Two balls splashed somewhere to starboard. The gunboat had fired across the bow.

'Captain?' The bosun's voice was thin, reaching him from one of the whaleboats, but even the distance did not hide the alarm the man felt. As would the others also.

Adamley picked up the leather cone of his loud-hailer and directed his voice forward. 'Cast off your lines, boys, and pull for shore.'

There was no escape, and he would

not ask his men to waste their lives needlessly. He turned the megaphone toward the rigging. 'Abandon ship, men. Abandon ship. Swim for shore, boys. Godspeed, and I thank you for your faithful service.'

He turned to his helmsman. 'You, too, Bedmer. Over the side with you.'

'What about you, Captain?'

'I've a task to perform before I go, son. We can't have the Federals taking all this French powder, can we? Nor the English rifles. Can't have them turned against the South, now, can we?'

'How are you — ?'

'Don't worry yourself about that, Bedmer. Over the side, now, to safety.'

The pair of Yankee gunboats thrashed nearer with truly alarming speed. Adamley only hoped he had time enough to do what must be done now.

His belly was cold with dread, but his determination did not flag. He knew his duty, and it would not have occurred to him to do less.

Cannon bellowed and flashed in the

night, and this time grapeshot and chain ripped through the rigging.

Adamley grabbed a packet containing the flint and steel used to fire the binnacle light and ran for the hatch covering the *Savannah Belle*'s hold.

An ax. A sledgehammer. Something. Anything. He kicked angrily at the roughly hewn staves of the powder cask he'd managed to free and drop onto the deck. He had to cut the cable cords of the netting that secured the cargo against the motion of the seas, and that had taken time.

He'd first tried hacking at it with the blade of a cutlass, but the cheap weapon was useful more as a bludgeon than a knife or sword. And his own fine sword was of course stored away in the chest in his cabin.

He'd scrambled up the ladder and into the open again in time to see the first of the Union gunboats close enough that a pair of their Marines stationed atop the deckhouse placed him under musket fire, damn them.

8

Adamley darted once more into the hold and sawed furiously at the cargo netting with his pocket knife. The knife was small, but at least it was sharp, and he got the job done. Got the powder cask down, but the cursed thing refused to break open. It fell from the top of the stack and only bounced when it hit the deck. And to add injury to that insult, it bounced sharply against his shin. The impact hurt, and he danced around on one leg for a moment in a macabre jig that he would have found humorous under any other circumstance.

But the cask. He had to break it. Had to expose the powder so he could scrape a spark and explode the cargo.

Couldn't let the damn Yankees have it. Could *not*.

He could hear now the thump and bang of grapples on the rails and the heavier impacts as the gunboat hull slammed hard against the side of the *Belle*. He could feel his dear ship lurch when the Yank rammed her.

No time. No time, he told himself.

Never mind the *Belle*. She was dead now or would be in a moment, and so would he. Just as soon as he broke the cask open.

He could hear shouted orders and the clatter of booted feet. A boarding party was on his decks. *Damn them. Damn them!*

He needed that ax. That sledge. Something. He had nothing. Nothing.

Frantic and furious, he kicked the side of the cask. He might as well have requested the staves to part for all the good that did. He grabbed up the cutlass he'd thrown aside minutes earlier and flailed wildly at the cask.

If he could only make the smallest opening.

Beating on the stubborn object did no good. He tried stabbing inside. He managed to gouge a few splinters out of the unyielding wood but no more than that.

In despair, he snatched up the lantern he'd carried into the hold and smashed it on the cask, freeing several cups of whale oil and creating a bright flame. All he needed was for the least hint of fire to reach the gunpowder that lay inside those barrel staves. One lick of flame, and the entire cargo would be blown to kingdom come and the *Belle* and he and the cursed damn Yankee Marines, too.

One smallest flame. That was all he needed.

Overhead, he heard shouts and curses.

'You. What are you doing down there?'

'Jesus, sar'n't, that looks like powder he's set afire.'

Alex Adamley felt a pummeling of his body as if powerful fists slammed into him, although no man stood near.

He could smell burnt gunpowder, and for one brief, joyous moment, he thought the cask had indeed caught fire and that his mission succeeded.

Then he realized the truth.

What he felt was the impact of bullets. What he smelled was the burning powder of the gunshots.

Oddly, he did not hear the gunfire that was killing him.

And there was no particular pain, save a dull throbbing in his left temple.

He opened his eyes and could see as clear as under a glass the flaming whale oil that lay on the deck only inches from his nose.

And why, he wondered, was he lying on this deck when there was yet so much to be done?

How had he gotten here? He did not remember falling. He still felt no pain; he saw only the fire. He felt now only the booted feet of the Marines as they threw him harshly aside and scrambled to smother the fire he'd started.

He wanted to reach out, wanted to stop them. He tried, but he could not empower his limbs to move and could force no words from his tongue.

No! he screamed in silent fury inside his head. *Don't stop it. Let it burn. No!*

The heel of a boot loomed huge in his vision, he felt a dull explosion against his skull, and he knew no more.

II

Death was, all in all, a rather pleasant experience. He felt no pain whatsoever. Nor, for that matter, any other sensation. None. It was as if he had no body. As if he were a spirit floating in a dark void with no earthly ties, no senses save . . . smell? He was almost certain he could smell tobacco. *Goodness. Who would have thought it?* Adamley found himself rather amused by the idea that the heavenly beings would partake of the weed. He'd been about to phrase that 'be addicted to,' but surely that would be an impossibility for heavenly creatures. Wouldn't it? Not that he —

'Goddammit!'

That did not sound heavenly in the slightest.

Alex Adamley opened his eyes. And sensation came flooding back to him.

He'd been sleeping, apparently. Just coming out of the pain-free, blessed healing of slumber.

With his abilities limited, he concentrated for a moment on the sense of scent. There was the tobacco as he'd already noted. A rather sour body odor that he hoped was not but feared indeed was coming from his own unwashed self. And a sharper, heavier stink that he'd smelled in the past on those occasions when he'd gone to visit his brother Donald back home in Savannah. It was a stench Alex associated with hospitals and death and so, yes, he probably was in the hospital ward of a Yank prison. It was the smell of rotting flesh . . . flesh that was rotting, that is, while yet a part of some poor dying soul's person. Oh yes. He'd smelled that before. Someone in this room or very close by it was well on the way toward death, the poor man.

Alex blinked and rolled his head slightly to one side, toward the window. There were no bars on the window, he noted. But then perhaps that was all elsewhere. Surrounding walls or that sort of thing.

Not that anyone need fear he would jump up and seek an escape. Not today.

'You're awake,' the same voice announced from the side of his bed toward the lone door.

Alex tried to respond, but his tongue and throat felt like total strangers to each other and to the instructions that flowed futilely from his brain. The best he could manage was to make his lips flutter in small movement.

He rolled his head — he was becoming quite adept at that, he thought — toward the voice.

A bearded face peered intently at him from a shockingly close distance. The man's breath smelled of tobacco smoke and . . . licorice? Possibly so.

'Welcome back to the living,' the

15

voice said. Alex focused his attention on the movement of the man's lips. That and the wiggling of his rather shaggy eyebrows seemed quite funny. Alex did not know why.

A hand floated into view and inexplicably lifted Alex's eyelids, first one and then the other.

'I must admit that I am amazed,' the voice said, the lips moving, tongue flexing, eyebrows waggling.

Alex closed his eyes. It all seemed overwhelming to him, and he was becoming weary.

'It appears to me, young man, that you shall live. Which is a mixed blessing. I am pleased on your behalf, of course, but distressed that now I must use the last of my laudanum to quiet you through the operation. Which wouldn't have been necessary, had you agreed to be a helpful chap and die on me. But no matter. It's an operation I've had to perform time and time again these past few months. At least you have the satisfaction of knowing I am well practiced, even if not quite so quick at it as some of my colleagues who followed the armies and worked right there at the battlefields. Too strenuous for me, of course. I stayed home, thinking to avoid the tragedies, but they followed me here. And now I have you to look after, don't I?'

The voice was not unkind, but in truth Alex was having difficulty understanding the meaning of the words that banged off his ears and spun away into the blackness that lay so close by.

'I'll need to find someone to help me strap you down and hold you,' the voice said, 'And then that limb can come off. Don't worry, though. I intend to take it at the joint, so there will be no need for the saw. You'll hardly feel it. Snip, zip, and away it goes, ha ha.'

Alex released his already tenuous hold on consciousness and let the blackness remove the pain again and all other sense along with it.

III

'I know you probably will not agree with me, Alex, but you are a remarkably fortunate young man.'

Alex sullenly turned his head away and said nothing in response to Dr Fredericks's cheerful comment. But then, what should he say? He felt neither fortunate nor a man. Not a whole one, at any rate. It would have been better had Fredericks simply allowed him to die. Save the painkillers for someone else who might appreciate them more.

It had been — what? — almost a month since the surgery. And he'd lain unconscious in a stupor for more than a week before that. The *Belle*. The *Belle!* Fredericks could tell him nothing about her.

'You have a robust constitution, Alex. That is a blessing, believe me. It amazes me, though. You carried the wounds of seven rifle balls. Two of them are still inside your body. At least one of those wounds should by all rights have been mortal. And that is without considering the gangrene that set in afterward. Yet here you sit, enjoying the sunshine in my garden, well on your way toward healing. Recovering nicely, although with no credit for that belonging to me. It is all you, Alex. Your vitality and your will to live.

'I have seen men suffer a scratch in the palm of their hand, sicken with disease, and die within days afterward. I've seen men and women, too, with no physical debilities known to medical science turn their faces to the wall and give up the spirit for no reason whatsoever. I have seen more death than I ever wanted to, Alex. Perhaps that is why your survival pleases me so very much.'

Alex looked at the old man, who was in the process of lighting his pipe, holding a magnifying glass to catch the slanting rays of afternoon sun and puffing quite furiously at the stem of his pipe. The poorly cured tobacco available these days was slow to take fire.

19

But then, all the best-quality weed had to be entrusted to the blockade runners so the nation could barter for the munitions and other matériel it so badly needed.

Ah, God, Alex thought. Here he sat, likely never again to cross the seas.

'I'm glad my survival is of interest to somebody,' Alex said, the bitterness lying heavy in his voice.

'Give yourself time. You've lost less than you think, my young friend.'

Involuntarily, his eyes were drawn downward to the empty sleeve. The right arm had been removed at the elbow. At least with the sleeve dangling, he did not have to see the bandages. He never had looked at the stump of truncated bone and flesh that made him less than a whole man. He could not bear to view it, could scarcely bring himself to acknowledge the truth of it.

'Your leg will heal, Alex,' Fredericks nattered on, his pipe spewing smoke now and sputtering so loudly that Alex could hear the moist sizzle from these several feet distant. 'Your strength will return. There is little you will not be able to do once you acclimate yourself to doing things with your left hand only.'

'Will I be able to climb the shrouds into a ship's rigging, Doctor? Can I haul an anchor or launch a boat? Can I?'

Fredericks looked more amused than confrontational, despite the tone of Alex's voice. 'It is my understanding, sir, that ships' captains do not perform those tasks, anyway.'

Alex turned away again. Captain of *what* ship, he wanted to snarl. The *Belle* represented the investment of everything he'd ever owned, everything he'd managed to accumulate, and everything he'd been able to borrow.

Now she was gone and all hope with her.

It wasn't only his own right arm that was missing. Along with that, the Yankees took his hopes, his fortune, and his future.

He had nothing.

Practically nothing. The house and contents. A few bonds. Little else. And what little he'd had was pledged to the holders of the notes he'd signed when he took ownership of the *Belle*.

Alex looked at the flat, wrinkled sleeve and thought again he would have been far better off had the Yankee balls taken his life along with everything else.

It was over. Everything except his life was over. And as for that . . . one more ball, this one properly placed, would take care of that unpleasant event.

IV

'No, Alex, sorry. I don't have a gun.' The old doctor shrugged and reached for the humidor that sat on his desk. 'I've been in the business of healing much too long to consider taking life instead. Cigar? No? Don't be shy, man. It would be difficult to cut the tip — so hard to manipulate the penknife properly with one hand, of course — but you can learn to bite the tip instead. You'll get the hang of it eventually.

'Well, eventually, that is, if you live long enough. Thinking of taking your own life, are you? I'll not provide you with a gun, Alex, but I will give you some advice. A man can always find a way to kill himself if he really wants. Are you *sure* you won't have one of these cigars? They aren't bad. Prewar, you see. A patient brought me seven of them as payment for services rendered. They're a little dry but otherwise very pleasant.'

'No, thank you.'

'As you wish, Alex. Where were we? Oh, yes. Your imminent demise. There is always hanging. Have you taught yourself to tie a knot yet? No? You must, of course. It can be done one-handed. You simply have to work at it until you learn. And a man can nearly always find a bit of rope if he wants. Climb onto something and step off. It looks to be an unpleasant death, since the fellow doesn't snap his neck as in a proper hanging. Dies by slow strangulation, you see. But it is effective. Did you know, by the way, that suicide by hanging is where we get the term 'kick the bucket'? It's true. Buckets are common articles to step from. And of course the legs thrashing about result in the bucket being kicked over as the lost soul is in the process of dying. Kicking the bucket in that instance is quite literally accurate. Hence the term.'

'You are not amusing me.'

'But I do not intend to amuse you, Alex. I am advising you. Now, there are no high places close by that you could jump from, and with one arm, you couldn't climb. Up a chimney, say, or a tree. No, I would say that for you jumping would be impractical. Drowning might be appropriate for a sailor. And you don't need deep water. The end of any self-respecting dock should do.

'Cutting oneself is overrated as a

means of suicide, Alex. It is much more difficult than laymen generally realize. And of course slitting the wrist is definitely out in your case.'

Alex quite involuntarily glanced down at the place where his right wrist should have been. And was not. He could not believe Fredericks was being so callous about this. Having saved his life, now the son of a bitch was advising him how he could take it back again. That seemed damned inconsiderate of the man.

'If you do decide to use a knife, cut the large artery here.' He laid his fingertips on the side of his throat. 'You'd have to slice deep and hard, but it can be done. It is a messy way to go, of course. Quarts and quarts of blood running all over. If you decide on that method, Alex, please consider whoever it is that will have to clean up after you. Go outside somewhere and choose a spot where the soil is porous. Sand, perhaps, or gravel so the blood will not pool and attract ants and rodents and what-not. And certainly not indoors.

The stains don't scrub away easily, and old blood leaves a very unpleasant odor behind. Do think about that sort of thing, will you?'

The doctor puffed on his cigar for a moment, then said, 'Have you considered your survivors, Alex? Burial arrangements? Filing of a last will and testament? That sort of thing? Not everyone does, and it can become a source of great distress for any family members left behind. Do you have family, Alex? You've never spoken of anyone.'

Alex said nothing, but he could not prevent a thought of his brother from flashing through his mind.

'May I make a suggestion, Alex? It is a decision that needn't be hurried. Before you commit yourself to the course, go home. Or wherever it is your family would be. Think about their future as well as your own. Then decide whatever it is you want to do.' Fredericks smiled through the veil of pale smoke that surrounded him.

'Tomorrow is soon enough, Alex. You needn't do anything today. And when tomorrow comes, well, tomorrow is still soon enough.'

Alex still said nothing. After a moment, the doctor laid his cigar aside and gruffly said, 'Now, if you would excuse me, young man, I have some things to do here. Go take a walk. The exercise will be good for you. And you still *can* walk, Alex. There are thousands who cannot. Now go on. Leave me alone for a while, please.'

Alex stood and fumbled for his crutch. Damn the old man, anyway. It wasn't his arm that was gone; he knew nothing about any of this. Nothing.

Damn him.

V

'Sit down, Alex. We need to have a talk.'

'Yes, sir?'

'You've been here now for the better part of three months.'

'Yes?'

'I think it is time for you to leave.'

Shock washed coldly through him. And fear. Adamley felt his gut tighten and his cheeks turn numb. 'I'm not ready,' he blurted.

'You would have been, had you tried,' Fredericks said bluntly. 'You've sat here basking in your misery. Pitying yourself. Attempting nothing.'

'I can't . . . I'm right-handed.'

'No, Alex, you are not. You were in the past. Not now.'

'But everything is so different. I can't write my own name. Can't tie a shoelace or slice a cheese. I'm not ready.'

'When was the last time you *tried* to tie a shoelace or slice a cheese, Alex?' The doctor paused. 'No answer? Of course not. Because you have none to give. You've counted on others to do everything for you. Well, that cannot continue. You remain here on my suffrage, Alex. That is now ending. I'll not waste any more time — or scarce food — on someone unwilling to help himself. I want you to leave, Alex. Go.'

'When?' His voice was a whisper.

'Tomorrow morning. First thing.'

'But I don't . . . I can't . . . '

'Tomorrow. First thing. Now, if you would please excuse me, I have other patients to tend to and other things to worry about.' The old man turned away and busied himself at something on the surface of his huge old roll-top.

Fear and bitterness alike gnawed at Alex's stomach as he stood and wedged the crutch into his left armpit. Tomorrow. It was too soon. Too soon.

VI

First thing. Did that mean he should go even before breakfast? That thought was as unnerving as the expulsion order. The thought of one missed meal . . . and no inkling of where the next might be found . . . Alex had never in his life had to worry about where food was to be found. In the kitchen. Belowdecks. Food was a commodity he'd always taken completely for granted. Now . . .

He rose with the dawn, as was his long habit, and sat on the side of the bed, the borrowed bed in Dr Fredericks' house, feeling alone and abused and . . . It was not fair. He hadn't recovered yet. He was not ready for this dismissal.

How was he supposed to travel? He had no ship, no carriage, no money. The Yanks had taken the *Belle*, and he'd had no money in hand, not aboard his own ship when at sea. There had been money in the chest in his cabin. Plenty of paper money issued from Richmond and some hard money, too. The English and the French dealt only in hard money, and a man had to carry specie with him if he intended to deal with them. He'd had probably two thousand left after paying for his cargo this time over. All of that was gone now, of course.

He supposed he still had some in his bank accounts back home. And his brother would have money. But now, here . . . he had nothing. Not even proper clothing. He wore the washed and patched shirt he'd had on when the boarding party shot him to pieces. And the canvas trousers he customarily wore when under way.

His shoes were cast-offs the doctor gave him as soon as he started getting around again, but those were ugly, ill-fitting articles unlike his own finely crafted Italian leather boots. Those he would never see again. Now they were on some Yankee's feet, he was sure, damn them all.

He'd lost considerable weight during his confinement, and the doctor compensated for that by adding some crudely fashioned galluses to hold his trousers up.

Oh, he was no doubt quite a sight. A right proper beggar with not even a hat to keep the sun from his eyes. Those few ragged articles of clothing and his crutch were all he possessed.

And Fredericks expected him to leave like this? The order was unconscionable. Cruel. And yet, to whom could he appeal? The Yankees? There were enough of them about. He saw them passing by on the road almost daily. Twice detachments of blue-clad soldiers stopped at the house for one reason or another. Alex had retreated to his bed when they came, leaving the doctor to treat them.

Alex sighed and stood, his stomach rumbling with hunger. He clumped slowly down the stairs and stood in the doorway of the breakfast room where a slave — except he supposed the blackamoor was not technically a slave any longer — was laying out bowls and wooden spoons for the doctor and two other patients in the makeshift hospital. Alex hadn't bothered to make their acquaintance and did not intend to now. But the porridge in the big pot smelled almighty good to him today whereas in recent weeks the sameness of the morning meals irritated.

'Good morning, Alex. Ready to go, are you?'

Alex hadn't seen Fredericks approaching. He grunted and cleared his throat.

'Go ahead. Have something to eat before you go.'

Alex felt a flush of gratitude for the meal and at the same time anger for this unfeeling exile into the unknown.

'Go on. Sit and eat.'

Alex ignored the other patients, both of them from some Virginia quartermaster unit pressed late into infantry service. He'd learned that much before the two of them accepted his disinterest and stopped trying to strike up conversations. Both of them were recovering from wounds. Both of them had all their limbs and all their faculties. Both of them would heal. Alex resented their recovery and was achingly aware of the empty sleeve that flapped loose where his arm and wrist and hand should have been.

He ate quickly, stuffing himself with

the oat porridge and reaching for more as soon as the first bowl was emptied. He might not eat again in days, perhaps.

Or never. And that might even be preferable, he thought.

He left the table only when he could hold no more. Fredericks followed him to the front door.

'I have something for you,' the doctor said, holding out a scuffed and soiled knapsack, probably something some past patient left behind. Or the property of a man now dead. Alex hesitated.

'There isn't much. I put in some scissors. You will find those useful to trim that beard and mustache you've grown. And I added a cheese for you to slice if you can bring yourself to learn how. I've also included a bill for my services, Alex. I expect you to pay it when you can. Now, goodbye, Alex. Godspeed.'

The door closed behind him, and Alex found himself alone. And more frightened than he'd been since he was a child.

A bill. My God, he thought. A bill for services rendered. Well, why not? The workman is entitled to the price of his hire. Isn't that what the Book says? Something like that, anyway. So all right. Fine. He would add Fredericks' bill to the long list of his obligations and pay it when he could. If he were still alive, that is.

As it was, he still owed one bank back home the balance of the loan he'd taken out to buy the *Belle*. And another bank where he'd borrowed capital to finance his latest — and last — cargo. Smuggling, it seemed, wasn't as lucrative as it was cracked up to be.

Oh, he supposed the captains who dealt largely in luxuries did well enough. Silks and needles and feathers for the ladies' hats commanded a fine price due to the shortage of supply. Alex rarely carried any such folderol in his hold. He'd always dealt in powder and musket caps and sturdy English rifles. Always sold to the Confederacy and received paper money and treasury bonds in return. Those he'd had to convert to specie at a bank in order to buy the next cargo, and the exchange rates were far from being favorable. This last trip, he'd sailed with 12,000 in hard money, but in order to secure that amount, he'd had to pay out 140,000 in paper currency and sign a note for another 100,000.

Alex fretted about finance and the future while he slowly walked eastward.

Without conscious thought, he traveled eastward. Toward the coast. Toward the salt smell of the sea. Toward . . . nothing. Nothing at all.

VII

A broadsheet posted along the street of a dreary little village somewhere along the Carolina coast declared the war was over. No details were offered apart from the claim that the end came at a courthouse in Virginia. Was that what it had come down to in the end? A court ruling?

Alex felt nothing. Not even any great amount of interest. Certainly he felt no elation. The thing that surprised him was that he felt no deep pain. It was simply a fact and one of less weight to him than the fact that his belly hurt from hunger. He'd finished the cheese yesterday and had nothing today but water. That was of more immediate concern to him than this proclamation that the agony was ended.

He saw an old man seated on a tree stump and walked over to him. 'Mister, I'd trade you this crutch for something to eat.' The crutch was not nearly so necessary as he'd thought. If anything, it got in the way. Now that he'd accepted the idea of walking, he was able to swing along at a steady pace without assistance from the crutch.

'Don't need a crutch. You can see that.'

'Sure.' Alex glanced back toward the post where the broadsheet was displayed. 'When'd they put that up?'

'Two, three days ago.'

'You think it's so?'

'Yeah, I'd think it's likely so.'

Alex sighed and shook his head. Now that he thought about it, there really was not all that much to be said. They'd given it their best. Their best was not good enough. Now . . . God knew what would come now.

Alex nodded to the old fellow and turned away.

'Mister,' the old man said behind him.

'Yes?'

'I got no money to give you, but I got this comb o' honey.' He pulled out a packet of oilskin and paper folded into a small square. 'Here.'

'It's a deal.' Alex offered the crutch to him.

'No swap. It's just . . . mister, I wish to Christ I did have a use for that thing. I'd give everything I have if my boy could use it. I'd give it all if he had no legs nor arms neither one.'

'He died?'

'At Malvern Hill.'

'I'm sorry.'

'Thank you. Now here. Take this.'

'But what about you?'

'Me and mine are fine, what there are of us. Now go on. Take this here an' go find your own people.'

Alex shrugged out of the knapsack slung over his shoulder, put the honeycomb inside, took the knapsack up again, then picked up the crutch and, using it as a walking staff rather than leaning on it, set off again. Southward. Toward home.

The war was over. He should care about that, of course. At the moment, that seemed too much to bother with.

VIII

God, damn them. Dear God, please damn them!

Destruction and burnt-out buildings marked their passage. They'd torn up and cut down, burned and ruined, despoiled and destroyed from sheer meanness. Without cause nor purpose.

Alex could understand them destroying railroads and warehouses and even wharves and moorings. All of that could be justified by the conduct of war against one's enemy.

Burning stores and homes, barns and carriage sheds . . . those were less comprehensible to him.

But to chop down fruit trees . . . that was pure malevolence, evil through and through. It could not have been an effort to deny food to an enemy. The trees in the yard where he now stood were little more than saplings, years away from bearing any peaches.

Yet the son of a bitch Yankees cut them down and left the slender branches lying where they fell.

They hadn't even cut the trees for firewood to warm themselves.

They acted out of cruelty. Nothing less.

Damn them, God. Please, he thought as he turned and trudged hopelessly on.

IX

The emptiness he felt in his belly had nothing to do with hunger if only because — quite oddly — it seemed that one's body became somehow inured to the pangs of hunger. At this point, Alex found that he had little interest in food. Being completely without food, it seemed, was much simpler and more comfortable than making do with little sustenance.

No, that he found comfortable enough now.

Yet his belly churned now and knotted into a tight fist.

He supposed he should have expected this. After all he'd seen in Carolina, after all the other wanton destruction, he really should have anticipated this.

Somehow he had not. Somehow he'd held a faint and fragile hope hidden deep within.

Somehow he'd thought there could be a homecoming.

He stood now, staring at burnt

timbers and cold ash and a trio of brick chimneys rising from this ruin like headstones above a gravesite.

And in a manner of speaking, perhaps that was appropriate, for here died the last of Alex's hopes.

The grand old house was gone. There was no sign of the people who'd once populated it.

He wanted to cry but knew he would not. Not even the release of tears was left to him now.

Everything was gone. Everything.

Damn them. He was not certain if he said the words aloud or heard them only inside.

Alex lifted his face to the breeze that swept in from the ocean and aloud repeated the phrase. 'Damn them, God. Please damn them.'

The request gave him no comfort as he left the street and walked slowly, unhappily toward the blackened, smoke-stinking rubble that once was his family home.

X

The lady was incredible. Judge Wilson's widow dressed, looked, and acted as if her life were unchanged and her home was as it appeared the last time Alex saw it. In truth, the Wilson home, the next one on the block to the Adamley place, consisted now of a scorched first floor front with blackened beams and partially burnt rubble behind it.

How the single wall remained standing, Alex could not imagine, but it did.

And where Mrs Wilson might be staying now . . . he had to assume she was living in the summer kitchen at the back of the property. That at least remained intact.

Alex stood at the steps of the broad porch — roofless now — that spread across the front of the ruins.

'It is nice to see you again, Alexander. Thank you for calling. Have you a card? I know Xenas will be pleased to receive it.' She smiled, her expression benign and guileless. The

43

gentleman she referred to was her husband. He'd been dead for a dozen years or more now, and the last Alex spoke with her, Clarice Wilson was in full control of her faculties.

She did not, he noticed, comment on the fact that he'd returned home only half a man. She ignored the empty sleeve where his right arm should have been.

But then, the people of the South were accustomed to seeing men without limbs nowadays. More than simply used to it, he guessed. There were so *many*.

'No, ma'am. I'm sorry. I have no card.'

'May I tell him that you've called, dear?'

'Please do.'

'Excuse me for not waking him. He does cherish his naps if you will recall.'

'Yes, ma'am. Please don't disturb him.'

'Thank you, Alexander.'

'Mrs Wilson, may I ask if you know where my brother is staying?'

She looked saddened. Sympathy and concern tugged at her features, and she reached out to lightly touch his wrist. 'I am sorry to be the one to tell you this, dear, but Donald is gone. There was a flux that swept through the city after the . . . the unpleasantness. Donald came down with it. But he didn't linger, dear. He did not suffer long before he passed.'

The words struck Alex like a spear. Donald. Safe, placid, stay-at-home Donald was the Adamley brother who failed to survive the war. Who would ever have thought it.

'Are you all right, dear? Would you care to come inside and let me make you a cup of tea?' Mrs Wilson took half a step backward and gestured with a flourish toward a grand manor that was no longer there.

Alex almost laughed out loud. Not with mirth but from the sheer absurdity of it all. 'No thank you, Mrs Wilson. You are very kind to offer.'

'Then please excuse me, Alexander. I

must go see to Xenas now.'

'Yes, ma'am.' He had no hat to tip so touched his forehead and backed away from the porch and the lady who had been so patient with him and Donald when they were boys. 'Thank you very much.'

'Come again, Alexander. I shall make your tea then.'

'Yes, ma'am. Thank you.' He turned and practically fled across the ragged, weedy lot that separated the ruins of the Wilson and the Adamley houses.

XI

The SOBs looted the place before they burned it. He did not know why that should seem so offensive to him now. Of course they had. What would be the fun otherwise? But finding the evidence of it now did bother him. It was, he supposed, the idea of some damn Yankee strangers pawing through the cherished and personal things of his family that rankled.

In the charcoal and ash heaps where the dining room and kitchen had been, he found spoons and ladles made of pewter and of steel. But the valuable silver was gone. They'd taken that.

Silver picture frames were gone as well. God alone knew what else was stolen before flames cleansed the place of the intruders' stench.

Alex poked through the ruins, using the tip end of his crutch to steady himself on the uncertain footing and to prod and pry at the wreckage.

He made his way straight across, as if walking through walls, but of course the walls no longer stood, to the chimney that marked for him the place where his father's study once was.

Somehow it was that room that represented to him the heart of what had been his home. Not his bedroom nor the playroom he and Donald shared. Not the kitchen where he'd always been able to find a treat or a hug or a cloth to wash his face and dry his tears. Not his mother's chamber where the rule was decorum and careful deportment. And certainly not the music room where he'd suffered through countless repetitions of those tedious, awful scales.

Somehow it was the library with his father's huge desk. And with the distinctive tobacco and whiskey scent of the towering old man himself. That was the heart of the house, and that was where Alex went now.

A skeletal remnant of the desk lay there, protruding from the ash and ugliness. It had been broken apart, of course. The violators would have expected to find there whatever cash the house may have contained.

They would have been disappointed.

Alex picked his way to the chimney and to the slate hearth. Some Yankee had gone to the trouble to batter the slate until it shattered. Looking, no doubt, for any hidden treasure box.

Alex almost laughed at the futility of that and at the anger that must have reddened the sweating, ugly face of that anonymous animal in blue, for there was no such box to find.

Not beneath the slate.

Instead, he used the tip of the crutch to sweep away an accumulation of cinders and charcoal from the right-hand base of the chimney, then captured the crutch in his right armpit — of late he was becoming quite adept at using his stump — and knelt to find and move the loose brick that was the trigger stone for the box the intruder failed to find.

He reached inside and dragged the steel box out. It was small. Perhaps three inches by five inches by twelve or fourteen. And it was light. It held little.

But whatever lay inside it was the entirety of Alex Adamley's worldly wealth.

All else was swept away, along with any joy in the present or hope for the future.

Careful lest he fall, Alex once again made his way through the rubble and waste, out onto cleaner ground and around to the back where the carriage house used to be and the woodshed still stood.

This, he reflected bitterly, was his homecoming.

XII

Even the wood that was always so carefully stacked was disarranged now, scattered in an untidy heap that filled the rickety woodshed. The detestable Yanks must even have taken the woodpile apart in their search for booty to steal.

Alex picked his way along the front wall and kicked pieces of stove wood aside to make a sort of nest for himself in the corner, then sank to the ground so he would be largely hidden behind the woodpile, should anyone look in.

It occurred to him only after he did this that he was quite automatically seeking to hide himself.

In all the days since he'd left the doctor, he had not bothered to give a moment's thought to robbery or personal safety. But then he had nothing that anyone might possibly want, his pockets being empty and his possessions limited to a castoff haversack, a pair of scissors, and the envelope containing Dr Fredericks's bill, as yet unopened.

Ironic that, having the strongbox from the library, he was now worrying about robbers.

Alex shrugged the haversack off his shoulders and laid it on his lap to act as a table, then set the enameled steel box on top of it.

He had little idea what he would find there. Over the years since their father died, Alex had added a few papers to the contents, and probably Donald did, too. Alex never had investigated the things left in the box, though. It would have seemed an intrusion. That was illogical now with his father gone and Donald also, of course.

But then, emotions are not necessarily logical.

He sighed now and unfastened the catch that held the box closed.

XIII

His own papers were few: the promissory notes he'd signed on the *Belle* and her last cargo, his commission into the navy of the Confederacy, a baptismal certificate, a diploma awarded by Emory College. That was the extent of it. The meager collection covered his lifespan.

It was, he realized, worth nothing now save memory. Still, memory was all he had. He transferred the thin packet into his haversack and looked further.

Donald's baptismal certificate was not present in the box. He must have kept it elsewhere, so presumably his personal papers were destroyed in the fire that ravished their home.

The only article Alex was sure his brother had added to the lockbox was a simple deed to something known as the

Culbertson Filing No. 8 in Bates Canyon, Colorado Territory. Whatever that was.

It took Alex a moment to realize what it was and then only when the name of the signatories jogged his memory. Before the war, Donald made a loan to a group of young men who had the intention of joining the then-current Pikes Peak gold rush. Alex assumed this deed of trust was their repayment of the debt. He could think of no other explanation, and Donald had never mentioned it to him.

God, he wished he could ask Donald about it now.

Alex shook his head and put the deed into the haversack with his own things.

Finally, he delved into the articles his father had placed in the box.

There was a trio of coins, twenty dollar gold pieces, which puzzled Alex as to why they might be there until he examined them more closely and realized the meaning they must have held for his father. The dates on the coins coincided with what must have been the three most significant dates in his father's life: his wedding and the birth of each of his two sons.

Alex keenly felt the pangs of loss when he recognized this. If only . . .

He frowned, scolding himself. It does a man no good to wish or to wonder. He can deal only with whatever is, not with what might have been. And Alex would never again see or speak with his parents or his brother. They were lost and gone, and that was that.

As for the coins, they were cash in hand and had to be viewed as such. When it came to his father's memories, or to Alex's own, there simply was no place for those. Not now.

He stuffed the coins into his trousers pockets and rummaged into the box further. There was little enough to be found there. A deed to the house. Worthless now, of course, except for the land value, and probably that was close to being worthless also.

Wedding and death certificates for his

parents, along with clippings from several newspapers relating to those events. Donald must have added the ones pertaining to their father; certainly Alex had not.

A copy of the lease for the building where their father once opened his ship's chandlery. That business was gone now, of course, closed early in the war after the blockade took effect. Alex had no idea if the building still stood, but the terms of the leasehold expired a good twenty years earlier. Their father had maintained the business location on the strength of a handshake during those latter years.

He returned his father's and brother's papers to the box and carefully latched it shut again.

Acting on impulse, he scooped out a depression in the soil of the woodshed floor and buried the lockbox there. He had no use for the things that remained inside it. But neither did anyone else, and it would have seemed an even greater intrusion upon his father and

Donald if strangers were allowed access to the box.

Alex shuddered. Sixty dollars in hard money and a deed to something called Culbertson Filing No. 8. That seemed to be the sum of his inheritance and his remaining worldly possessions.

He closed his eyes and lay down, hidden behind the scattered stove wood should any unwelcome eyes pry. It was not particularly late in the day, but he had no desire to venture outside again. Not just now. Tomorrow would surely be soon enough.

XIV

It was the little things, Alex was learning, that creep upon a man to taunt and dismay and remind him of things that no longer were.

The banker was a good and decent man and would give no deliberate affront. He simply did not notice when Alex first entered his office. The gentleman came round his desk and extended his hand in welcome, not seeing that Alex's sleeve was empty.

And Alex, unthinking, gave response to thirty-two years of training and habit. Alex tried to take that offered hand.

He swung his stump forward. Then recoiled in horror when he realized what he'd done while poor Mr Warren saw his gaffe and jerked his own hand back. 'I . . . I'm sorry.' Both spoke the identical words and at almost the same exact moment.

'Forgive me,' the banker hurriedly added. 'I didn't . . . see.' He finished the apology lamely, eyes locked on the dangling cloth where a hand and forearm should have been.

'No, I . . . ' Alex shook his head and pressed the stump tight against his ribs as if that would hide its ugliness.

'Come sit down. Over here. Please.' Mr Warren treated him now as if he were an invalid, taking his elbow — the intact one — shepherding Alex to a chair, even helping to lower Alex into the chair.

And — quite incomprehensibly as to the reason, but it was something Alex had encountered from others before from time to time, and would so do again — the gentleman raised the volume of his voice slightly and spoke with slow deliberation. As if Alex's deformity extended somehow to his hearing or to his mind.

'What may I do for you, Mr . . . ' He paused for a moment, searching for the name, then visibly relaxed as it came to him. 'Mr Adamley?' He looked rather proud of himself to have come up with it, then remembered the rest and amended the greeting, 'Or, um, Captain Adamley, I should say.'

'I've come to discuss my notes, Mr Warren. I owe, if I remember correctly, sir, something on the order of three thousand five hundred.'

'I do not have the exact figure in memory of course, Captain, but I am sure your recollection will be adequate for the moment. Please go on.'

'My ship is gone, sir. So is everything else I owned or hoped to.' He explained the circumstances as dispassionately as he could, then said, 'I am reduced to these.' He took out the papers that represented the promissory notes and — the only one of any potential value whatsoever — the deed to the family home.

'The house was destroyed, sir, but surely the property will be worth something. If not today then someday. The city hasn't been all that badly damaged, I've noticed. The Navy Yard is gone. But the port will still be vital. The city will go forward. In addition to this, there was a savings account. It should hold a few hundred. I don't remember exactly. And there should be a balance remaining on the draft I used to make up my last outbound cargo. Both of those can be applied to my indebtedness, I should think. I have . . . nothing else of value.'

He'd given long thought to the three

coins left by his father. They would not have been so much as a pittance against his debt, but they were all he had to sustain himself until . . . until he decided whether to die or to live and if to live then for what purpose.

The banker examined the things Alex gave him, then shrugged. 'I commend your honesty, Captain Adamley. I doubt we will hear from most of our debtors. If you would excuse me for a minute, I will have a bill of sale prepared for your signature and a power of attorney so we can attach your accounts without asking for a court order. I assume that will be acceptable to you?'

'Yes, sir. Quite. Thank you.'

Warren rose and left the small office, and Alex squirmed uncomfortably on the hard visitor's chair.

He'd not signed anything, nor tried to write anything whatsoever, since — *why* was it so damned difficult to say to himself anyway? — since the arm was taken from him. Since he became less than whole. Since he became less than a man.

When the banker returned with the documents, he brought pen and ink with which to sign them. Alex had to shift the paper this way and that while he struggled to find an angle that he could approach with this unfamiliar hand. He finally managed to scratch out a stiff and wooden approximation of the signature that once was his. His fingers felt like pegs or small sausages on the barrel of the pen, and the ink overflowed in dark puddles where he pressed too hard against the paper. Even so, he got the job done and laid the pen down.

Mr Warren carefully blotted the result without comment and set the bill of sale aside to dry while he ushered Alex quickly and firmly out of the office and away from the bank.

Alex gathered he was no longer so welcome here as a potential customer as once he'd been. Somehow that revelation came as no great surprise.

But that was all right. He'd done what he could to liquidate the last of his worldly obligations.

Now he was free to . . .

To do what? He had no earthly idea. The future, whatever of it there proved to be, lay empty and useless before him.

But he most certainly was free to pursue that future. Unless he chose otherwise.

He shifted the haversack higher onto his shoulder and began walking. The one and only thing he was sure of was that by nightfall he wanted to be out of the reach of salt air.

He wanted no more of the reminders that came with the smell of the sea.

He turned his face westward and again using his crutch as a walking stick set out without purpose. Or destination. Or hope.

After a little while, it occurred to him that no matter what happened now, he could not be disappointed. For he expected nothing and thus could not find less than what he sought.

His pace picked up a little once that came into his mind, and he swung along the roadway with something closer to cheerfulness than he'd experienced since the night those damnable Yankees closed on the old *Belle*.

Why hell, he was almost willing to concede that it was a lovely spring day, and he was able to stride out now with a bit of a bounce in his step.

XV

'Sit down, mister. Join us.' The man was one of five who were gathered around the remains of what once must have been a fine home. They were seated on the stumps and logs of pecan trees that had been chopped down for the sheer meanness of it. 'Down to that end of the garden patch you might find some spuds or some sweet taters. No, you don't look for 'em like that, mister. They grow underneath the ground. Use the tip end o' that crutch o' yours to kinda gouge around in the dirt and see if you can pry something to the surface. There! That's right. Now all you got t' do is rub some of that dirt off it and you got you a lunch. Don't worry 'bout the skin. It's eatable. Just wipe the dirt an' have at 'er, if you see what I mean. Right. Like that. Say now. Where was it you said you was bound?'

Alex paused, his mouth filled with the crisply delicious raw potato, a familiar enough food, although not one he'd ever tried prepared in this manner. As it was, he could taste the soil on the skin almost as strongly as the meat of the thing.

He blinked. 'I, uh . . . Colorado Territory,' he answered, thinking about the deed his brother had possessed. He had no idea exactly where or exactly what Culbertson Filing No. 8 would be. But as Donald's heir, he did seem to own it, whatever it was, and he supposed he should have a destination in mind.

The helpful bummer, who had all his

major limbs intact but was scarred on the left side of his face and neck as if he'd been in a fire, nodded twice and belched once. 'That's a long way, mister.'

'Is it?' Alex honestly had no idea. Colorado Territory was in the West. That was the extent of his knowledge on the subject.

The bummer looked at him and chuckled, then seemed to think better of that and shrugged instead.

'You don't even know where Colorado is, do you?' Alex shook his head.

'It's the far end of what used t' be called Kansas Territory. They carved off the west half. That's Colorado. You know where Kansas is?'

Alex shook his head again.

'It's way the hell and gone the other side of the Mississippi River. West of the Missouri River, even. Kansas is west of Missouri. Colorado is west of Kansas. It's an awful long way off from here, I'm telling you.'

Alex shrugged. 'I sure to God have

no reason to stay here. I might as well go to Colorado.'

'How are you gonna get there?'

That was something else he hadn't really thought about. 'Walk, I suppose.'

'It's too far to walk.'

'All right. I won't walk to Colorado. I'll walk down the road here a few miles. Then tomorrow I'll do the same. If that gets me to Colorado, well, there's no harm in that, right?'

For the first time, the scarred bummer grinned. 'Now, mister, that attitude is considerable better. I like that.'

Alex said nothing, so the bummer went on without encouragement. 'I been walking south for the better part of a month myself. Got put out of a Yankee prison camp up in New York state. They gave me half a blanket and a loaf of bread and told me to go home. God knows if I got a home to go to, but that's where I'm headed. Point is, soldier, I've learned a few things along the way.

'First, stay out of the path the Yankee armies took. Those sons of bitches stole everything they could carry and burned whatever they couldn't fit into a haversack. Folks will treat you kindly along the way, but if they got nothing to share, they won't be able to feed you. And you, you can't offer to do work to pay for your meal, so you might as well get used to having an empty belly.

'Shortest way from here west would be to go through Atlanta, but you don't want to do that. There's naught on that road but embers and hard feelings. Best you swing to the south far enough to get clear of the path Sherman's thieves took coming down here.

'If you got any money — and mind that I'm not asking if you do — you might think about buying a horse. That'd be the best way to travel. My advice to you is, don't do that. Maybe you could handle saddling and bridling and keeping a horse if you're adept with that one hand, but even if you could do it, don't. A man with a horse presents himself as having something worth stealing. And on the roads you'll be using, a man who looks like a victim is soon enough going to be one. You hear what I'm telling you, mister?'

'I hear you.' The advice was superfluous. Alex had never been on a horse in his life and had no desire to do so. And he was certain he could not do all that saddle and harness stuff, whatever it was called, with only one hand. No, riding was out of the question anyway. But probably this fellow knew what he was talking about when it came to being cautious about potential robbers. A one-armed man would surely present an easy target if anyone thought he had wherewithal worth stealing.

'Another real important thing is that you should trust in the decency of the folks you'll meet. Even up North, the farmers saw that I'm Southren but were kind to me in spite of it. Fella named DeShong in Pennsylvania took me into his home and gave me these shoes to wear and good food in my belly. Fella named Mellott said he needed a pad to go under his saddle and wondered would I swap him my blanket half for the good wool blanket I got with me now. Mister, that man hadn't saddle horse anywhere on his farm. But I sleep warm every night now, thanks to him.

'What I'm saying is, trust to the goodness of the folks along your way, and you can't go wrong. You know?'

Alex looked at him. 'I don't know. Could be I'd be better off to find some of the other kind and let them do what I don't seem to have the courage for myself.'

'If it's trouble you really want, mister, you'll have plenty of opportunity to find it. But you'll have to go looking for it, because generally speaking, folks are good and decent and kind. You'll see.'

Alex grunted. After a while, the bummer stood, the cartilage in his knees crackling, and began walking back toward the spot where he'd made his bed.

'Mister.'

The bummer stopped, turned his head.

'Thank you.'

The man nodded solemnly and went on.

When Alex woke in the morning, the bummer had already rolled his blanket and left.

2

I

Half a lifetime spent at sea, dashing up ratlines and handling sails aloft and treading the hard planks of a dozen decks will not prepare a man for walking barefoot across half a continent.

It was a discovery Alex made somewhere in Alabama when the secondhand shoes provided by Dr Fredericks quietly — and rather messily — gave up the ghost in a red clay mud puddle.

It occurred to him some miles afterward that this, finally, was a misery that could not be attributed to the loss of his arm. And thank goodness he still had his feet to carry him forward.

Alex had been lean before. Now he was gaunt. And ragged. He had no change of clothing that would permit him to wash one set while he wore the other. The best he could manage toward cleanliness was to step fully clothed into whatever standing water was available and wallow himself about in it until the surface dust at least was sluiced away.

As for personal cleanliness, that was even more difficult. Not that he possessed any soap, but on those few occasions when a meal was offered and a washstand to go with it, he found it nearly impossible at first for one hand to clean itself. By trial and error, largely error, he learned to roll the empty sleeve up past his stump, daub soap onto that, and then rub the stump with his remaining hand.

The experience was unsettling the first few times. Until then he had done his best to pretend the bony, ugly stump did not really exist. Having to use it, having to touch it, made him perforce acknowledge it. He did so by necessity alone, a creepy-crawly sensation filling his gut each time he touched the awful, empty thing.

Most experiences were not so wrenching, but the adjustments were disturbing, nonetheless. It was the little things that would sneak up on him as unexpected reminders and newfound awkwardness.

Tightening a belt was difficult, the solution being to thread it onto his trousers the wrong way through so he could pull it with his left hand rather than having to reach across his belly and tug.

Tying a knot was nigh impossible as was any sort of shaving. The scissors served to trim his beard, but even that was difficult, the angles being awkward to him and his left hand having no natural dexterity whatsoever.

Fastening buttons was a time consuming, intense chore.

Tucking the right side of his shirttail inside his trousers was difficult and often only partially accomplished.

His right-side trouser pocket was useless, for he could not reach into it while wearing his britches.

Crushing the end of a twig so he

could scrub his teeth with it was at first insurmountably hard. A man with two hands can simply snap off the twig, hold it against something solid, and bash the end with a rock or other substantial object. But how do you hold it and at the same time strike it if you have only one hand to work with? Alex learned to make do by biting the end of a twig until the fibers crushed, then using that with a pinch of salt or clay to polish his teeth.

Cutting meat — not that he frequently had meat that required cutting — was even worse. Anything he ate had to be boiled soft enough to need no cutting. Either that or he had to pick it up and tear at it with his teeth like a wild animal gnawing a dead thing, for he had no way to hold an object in place while he sawed or stabbed or pulled at it.

The bummer back in Georgia had been right about one thing, though. The people he encountered were decent and kind and generous to a fault. Most of them had little more than he did. But what little they had they were willing to share with him.

They called him Soldier — he quickly gave up trying to correct that as so few had any knowledge of the maritime services — and, worse, they called him Hero. The kindness they showed him was embarrassing, for he'd done nothing to deserve it. He'd fought in no battles, vanquished no enemies, marched to no one's drum. Yet the common people of the South saw in him a reflection of the sons and husbands and brothers who would not be coming home, and they shared with this stranger whatever they had to offer.

Trust to the goodness of folks. The bummer had been very right about that.

Still using the crutch for a walking stick, Alex marched on toward each evening's setting sun.

II

'Adamley.'

'Yes, Captain?' Captain. There wasn't a ship nor a sea nearer than two thousand miles, Alex guessed, but this man was called Captain, nonetheless. Captain of a train of heavy freight wagons bound for Santa Fe. Alex had been in their company since meeting them all the way back east in Arkansas. After the first two weeks, they'd taken him on as a helper. Despite his limitations, he'd been able to help feed the oxen and watch over them through the night while sleeping atop a wagon during the days. His pay was in food, and the arrangement seemed satisfactory to all. Most assuredly he was pleased with it.

'We'll be reaching El Pueblo sometime tomorrow. From there we turn south, across Raton Pass and down into New Mexico, then on to the capital. I want you to know you're welcome to stay with us. In fact, I hope you will.

76

Colorado Territory is hard country, man. Hard winters and hard men alike. And if you don't mind me saying so, it's no country for a man who can't . . . well . . . stand up for himself. If you see what I mean.'

'I see what you're saying, Captain, and it's kind of you. I appreciate the concern and the decency you've shown me. But I expect I'll go on to Cherry Creek.'

'Is that where your brother's property is?'

'I don't know. The deed says Bates Canyon, wherever that is, but I remember him talking about Cherry Creek. I believe that's where he said his friends were going to prospect.'

The freighter shook his head. 'Cherry Creek is known as Denver City these days, Alex, but I've never heard of Bates Canyon. I hope . . . I hope you're not in for a disappointment.'

'How can I be disappointed when I have no expectations?' Alex returned. He thought but did not add that if all else failed, he still had that one final option. And judging by the mountains he'd so plainly been seeing ahead of them for the past week and more, in Colorado Territory there were plenty of high places a man could walk to if it came to that.

'Yes, well, I wanted you to know ahead of time so you can think this over. I still believe it would be best for you to come along to Santa Fe with us. I hope you'll change your mind.'

'I won't. But I thank you.'

The burly, kindhearted fellow sighed. 'All right then. As you wish. But mind you come speak with me before you leave the train. I'll be wanting to give you a few items to add to your load.'

'I wouldn't think of leaving without thanking you, Captain.'

'Yes, well, tomorrow then. For now, you'd best climb up top of some rig and get yourself some shut-eye.'

'Yes, sir. I'll do that.' Alex waited for the wagon driven by Hector Guzman to reach him, then grabbed the side of the driving box and stepped up onto a wooden block old Hector had added to his wagon for his own use in climbing onto the awkwardly high rig. The step made Hector's wagon much easier to get into than any of the others, and Alex generally chose it to sleep on.

Once aboard the moving wagon, he passed a few words with Hector — very few, as Hector had little English and Alex no Spanish whatsoever — then stood on the seat and persistently if with some difficulty clambered over the front bow and onto the canvas roof. The depression between bows formed a rather comfortable hammock, the movement of the wagon reminding him strongly of the feel of a ship in choppy seas.

He fell asleep quickly and dreamed of high places.

III

'I can't accept this,' Alex protested.
'Of course you can.'

'But I didn't earn it.'

The captain of the freight train cocked his head to one side and gave Alex a searching look. 'You mean that, don't you?'

'Pardon me?'

'You really think you haven't earned your way all these weeks past.'

'Yes. I think exactly that. For it is true. I've been a burden to you, and — '

'Alex, you've worked harder than any other man on this train. You've fed and watered and tended and herded and I never once heard a word of complaint or self-pity from you. Why do you think I want you to stay with my train, man? You're dependable, and you're smart. Given a little time to learn, you could lead trains yourself. I could teach you, Alex. Another year or two, and I could expand my freight line. You could take over one train, and I'd handle another. I've had that in mind for days now. Still do. Think about it, Alex.'

He looked down at the empty, dangling sleeve.

'That has nothing to do with it,' the freighter declared. 'It limits your activities some. But not your abilities.'

Alex blinked. It was an interesting way to put it, he thought. 'You are a kind man,' he said.

'Kindness has nothing to do with it, either. It's self-interest, Alex. You could expand my earnings by plenty. I wish you'd stay.'

Alex shook his head.

The captain sighed. 'Your choice, of course. Now take this pay. You've earned it.'

'But I — '

'Take it.' The freighter bypassed Alex's reluctant palm and dropped some coins into his right-hand pants pocket, where it was not possible for Alex to reach and return them. 'There, damn it,' he said with a smile.

'Thank you.' Alex felt something of a fraud, however. He still had two of the twenty-dollar pieces he'd brought away from home all the way back in Georgia. Concerned about loss or thievery, he'd snipped open a seam in the waistband of his trousers and slipped the coins in there for safekeeping until he reached Cherry Creek. He'd managed to cross half the continent with the other twenty dollars and a great deal of kindness from strangers, including this gentleman. 'Captain, thank you.'

'If you change your mind, Alex, come to Santa Fe. The offer stands.'

'You can't know how much that means to me.'

The older man shrugged. 'Like I said, Alex. It's pure self-interest. I could use your help. Keep it in mind, and God speed.'

'Goodbye, sir.' Alex turned north along what the captain said was Fountain Creek, while from here the wagons would travel south across a distant mountain and on down to Santa Fe.

To reach Cherry Creek — no, Denver City it was called now, and he should get used to thinking of it that way — to reach Denver City, all he had to do was walk north close beside the

Front Range mountains. He couldn't miss it. Or so they said.

Alex picked up his crutch, still recognizable as such although for a long time now he'd used it only as a staff or walking stick, and began the final leg of his long journey.

IV

Indians! Imagine. He'd come all this way, weeks and weeks traversing the great American desert with the freight train, right through the heart of what they called the Indian Nations or the Five Civilized Tribes . . . and he had never seen an Indian.

Until now.

Not that they were so very much to look at. They were swarthy and squat and dressed as if a parody of Lo! the Poor Indian, wearing scraps and tatters and bits of filthy blanket.

There were a dozen or more of them, mostly women and children, camped in the shade of some large trees close by the creek.

Alex altered his course so as to come closer for a better look. A handful of scruffy dogs saw him first and set up a howling that brought a trio of scowling men into view while the women quickly gathered up the children and ushered them out of sight.

'Sorry for all the commotion,' Alex said as he entered the camp.

The Indian men — braves, he supposed they should be called, or bucks . . . certainly they did not look like warriors — were grease smeared and nearly naked. One of them held an ax as if it were a weapon, while the other two scurried to snatch up stones large and jagged enough to do a man damage if struck with one.

'It's all right,' Alex assured them. 'I didn't come here to cause you any trouble. I was just curious. To tell you the truth, I've never seen an, uh, Indian. Before now, I mean.'

The men glared at him and spoke

among themselves, the one with the ax being the loudest and most belligerent sounding of them.

A fat and homely Indian woman emerged from one of the two conical tents that appeared to serve as housing for all parties of this little band. She came forward and said something to the men, then took a moment to look Alex over stem to stern before she grunted something and turned again to speak with the menfolk.

The men seemed not to like what she was saying, but whatever the message, they quite obviously acquiesced, for they quit glaring at Alex and walked away downstream, back in the direction of El Pueblo and the now-distant Arkansas River.

When the men were out of sight, the woman motioned for Alex to follow and led him inside one of the tents where an iron pot was emitting steam and a perfectly mouthwatering aroma from its spot over a fire set in the center of the tall tent.

Outdoors, the camp smelled of smoke and ash and body wastes, both human and animal, but inside the tent, the aroma was delightful.

The interior of the tent was larger than it appeared from the outside and was appointed with hides and woolen blankets on the floor, woven backrests for sitting, and piles of furs and more blankets arranged around the circular wall to form beds. Alex could see wide, sparkling eyes staring at him from within and behind the bed mounds. Those would be the children, he presumed, although in the dim interior of the tent, the visibility was not particularly good.

Three more women squatted close to the stew pot. One of these stood and fetched a wooden bowl from a leather box hanging from one of the support poles. She dipped the bowl into the stew and handed it to Alex while the first woman motioned that he should help himself to a seat beside the fire.

He sat cross-legged where she indicated and, lacking any utensils to eat with, drank from the side of the bowl.

The stew tasted even better than it smelled. It was rich with a pale, shredded meat. Not beef, he was sure, and not horse, either, for he'd eaten a good many oddities in the course of his travels to far places. He was fairly sure he'd never encountered this dish before, but whatever it was, he liked it. It was thickened somehow and contained potato-like tubers and greens and what he took to be onions, although of a variety he was not familiar with. In all, the meal was excellent.

'Very good. Thank you.' He smiled and lifted the bowl to indicate what he meant. The women smiled back and motioned for him to continue. And so he did. He ate his fill and thanked his hostesses repeatedly.

When he was done, he bowed politely to the ladies, cast a smile and a wave in the direction of the tittering but unseen children, who were hiding around the fringes of the tent, and went back outside.

'You are very kind,' he told the women again and again.

There was no sign of the men, so he could not thank them also. He bowed to the women a final time and turned to go, but one of the women stopped him with a touch on his elbow. She motioned for him to wait, then darted back inside the tent. When she emerged a moment later, she was carrying something.

Something live and squirming, he saw. She had a puppy in her hands, a smooth-haired little creature of nondescript brown with black eyebrows and a white patch on its chest.

The woman stepped behind Alex, where he could feel her unstrapping his haversack and stuffing the puppy inside.

A gift. How about that. He smiled and laughed and thanked her all over again. A puppy. He hadn't had a dog since he was not much bigger than this pup was now. And hadn't that been a very long time ago.

'Thank you, thank you.'

All three women nodded and smiled, and before the moment became too awkwardly long, Alex took his leave of the camp of friendly Indians and went on his way.

V

'You are one dumb and lucky son of a bitch,' the Colorado City storekeeper exclaimed.

Alex had stopped at the establishment to buy a few foodstuffs and got to talking to the gent about the puppy that followed his every footstep, its tail wagging so hard that its fat little butt was wagged along with the whipping tail.

'What d'you mean by that?'

'I mean you're just damned lucky those Injuns didn't kill you, that's what I mean.'

'Oh, pshaw. They were perfectly harmless.'

'Mister, you came up here from El Pueblo, right?'

'Yes, I did.'

'That whole settlement was pretty nigh wiped out by those Injuns, mister. Christmastime, it was, not six, seven years ago, something like that. The Injuns was nice and friendly and some of them was being taught to be Christian and everything. Come the holiday, they was invited to join in, eating and singing and all. Well, they joined in, all right. They took clubs and knives and axes and stuff and they killed . . . God, I don't remember how many white Christian people they massacred. Killed everybody they could catch, then burned the settlement to the ground. Harmless? Don't you believe it. I dunno what kept you alive, mister, but it wasn't from them Injuns being harmless.' The storekeeper laughed.

'And the gift they gave you?' He pointed to the pup that was tugging on the already ragged hem of Alex's right trouser leg. 'That pup was intended for traveling supplies. They expected you to whack it in the head and have it for your supper.'

'You don't mean — '

'Oh, but I do mean,' the storekeeper assured him.

Alex thought back to the stew he'd enjoyed there at the Indian camp. The meat was . . . he shuddered. Didn't want to think about it.

'Give me a couple pounds of rice, please,' he said, wanting to change the subject.

'I got some canned milk,' the storekeep suggested.

'No, thanks.' He didn't cope very well with cans, it being too difficult to open one with no way to hold it firmly down while he used an opener. 'But if you have any dried fish, I could use some of that.'

'No such thing as that around here, mister, but I have some jerked buffalo. It's kind of like dried beef.'

'All right, let me have a pound or so of that, too, please. And tea. Do you have any tea?' He went on with his shopping, determined not to think back to that aromatic stew pot and the meat that was in it.

VI

'You,' Alex said, 'are going to have to do your own walking. You're too dang heavy for me to carry.'

The pup did not seem at all abashed. It scrambled awkwardly into his lap and laid its chin on his wrist. Alex laughed and scratched the fat little thing behind its ears.

He — they — had stopped for the night in a copse of mixed pine and juniper and scrub oak north of Colorado City. He preferred to make his camps close to scrub oak, because there was always a tangle of twigs and dry leaf litter caught inside the base of the oak clumps. He could gather his tinder and kindling by the handful and pull thicker branches free with one hand also.

The store he'd stopped at earlier carried sulphur matches, so he hadn't needed to stop early enough to catch afternoon sunlight in his magnifying glass in order to start a fire. That was fortunate, because this close to the mountain wall on his left, the sun disappeared early, making it impossible to start a fire with sunlight past four or five in the afternoon.

'I hope you like rice,' Alex told the squirming, happy pup, 'because that's what we're having.'

Over the past several months, he'd assembled a ragtag collection of discarded cans of various sizes that he used for cooking, as drinking vessels, whatever. The largest now had water and half a cup or so of rice bubbling in it while a smaller can held coffee. The aroma coming off the coffee was beginning to smell awfully good.

'No coffee for you, though,' he

warned. 'It'd stunt your growth.'

The pup did not seem to mind. It licked his hand and rolled onto its back, offering its belly to be scratched. Which Alex did.

'I suppose you're going to want to sleep under the covers again tonight,' Alex grumbled aloud in a voice that was anything but complaining. 'All right. But if you pass wind, out you go.' He laughed, the sound causing the pup to stop its wriggling and peek at him. 'You heard me. Mind your manners. Consider yourself warned.'

It occurred to him that the sensible course probably would have been for him to stay with the freight wagons. Go to Santa Fe and try to make a life there.

He sighed. There really wasn't any *reason* to keep on to Denver City.

Except that deed in his haversack was the only thing he owned that held any continuity with the past and with his family.

Perhaps that was reason enough. That and the simple stubbornness that made him hold to a goal once set. Wind and tide might've made him alter course in his pursuit of a destination, but he'd always persevered to whatever port he intended to reach.

'Get down now,' he told the pup. 'I think our supper is ready.'

VII

The man shook his head and idly scratched under his chin. 'Bates Canyon, you said?'

'That's right.'

The fellow shook his head again. 'No, sir, I can't say as I've ever heard of it. Sorry.'

'Look, I know it exists. I have a deed to some property there.'

'I'm sorry. I wish I could help you.'

Alex sighed. 'If a freight agent never heard of it . . . ' He'd come to the freight agency partially because of the helpfulness he'd found among freighters and bullwhackers on the long way westward and partially on the theory that anyone who hauled goods locally should surely know the locale.

'I'll tell you what I'd suggest,' the agent said. 'That would be either the courthouse or the post office. And to tell you the truth, I think I'd ask at the post office first. It wouldn't do you any good to ask at the county courthouse if your place is outside the county, but the post office ought to know pretty near every nook and cranny where a man could take up residence.' The man smiled. 'And some of those places will purely amaze you when you see them, mister. Some places I've seen drifts bored straight into the middle of a cliff face, so the men working the claim had to either cut stairsteps into live rock or let themselves down by ropes from overhead just to reach their vein. That part of it I can accept, for I know a man will do almost anything he has to t' get his ore out. The thing that really baffles me, though, is how the fella found that vein in the first place.' He shook his head again, still smiling.

'The post office,' Alex said, returning to his own topic of interest. 'That's a good idea. Thanks.' He gave a tug to the scrap of twine he was using as a leash for the pup and dragged the inquisitive little thing away from a bit of discarded paper that was the focus of its attention at that moment. It had taken Alex twenty minutes and a considerable amount of cussing and fuming to tie the twine in place, but he'd gotten it done. Now that they'd reached the bustling activity of Denver City, he didn't want to take a chance on losing the puppy or letting it run under the wheels of a passing wagon.

'It's a pretty long way to the post office, mister,' the freight agent warned him. 'It's all the way over on the hill where the capitol and territorial buildings are.'

'Then it's a good thing I'm not on a tight schedule, isn't it,' Alex said on his way out the door.

VIII

'Bates Canyon. Now there's a name I haven't heard in a long time,' the postal worker mused. 'Not for years.'

This was the third person Alex spoke with at the Denver City Post Office and the one the others said had been here the longest, his tenure dating back to the earliest days of the Cherry Creek gold rush that led to the creation of the city.

Or village, Alex thought. Denver might call itself a city, but he judged it contained but a few thousand souls. To someone from Savannah — and moreover to someone familiar with truly old and magnificent cities like London and Antwerp and Marseilles — Denver City seemed small beer.

Still and all, this gentleman was an

old-timer by local standards, and that was what counted at the moment.

'Bates Canyon is . . . let me see if I remember . . . it's pretty far beyond Golden, I think. Up above Georgetown and Idaho Springs. There never was a post office there, but I do remember some mail being addressed to it.' He stared off into space for a moment while he tried to remember. 'I think everything for that area now is addressed to Holihan. But I don't know for sure if Holihan is the same place or just the nearest to it with an established post office.'

'How can I reach this Holihan place?' Alex asked.

The man pointed out the west-facing doorway. 'You see those mountains out there? Just head straight for them and follow the road when you get there.'

'You've been a big help. Thanks.'

'My pleasure, mister. It's the least I can do. After all, you and men like you helped keep this country together.'

Alex frowned at the thought that he'd

been mistaken for a plundering, cowardly damn Yankee, but he did not want to get into an argument with the postal worker. He turned and got the hell out of there.

IX

The clerk in the mercantile eyed Alex with obvious skepticism. 'Mister, it's none of my business, but prospecting isn't a good prospect right now. If you'll pardon the levity. I mean, even for a man with two good hands, there just isn't much new being found these days. And, well, you just aren't gonna be able to hire on at any of the established mines. I don't know what all you may've heard. It's true that an able-bodied man can find good work up there. Three dollars a day, that's the going wage. But you . . . ' He shook his head. 'I don't think you'll find much.' His expression brightened. 'Unless you have a skill that's in demand. What is it you do, if you don't mind me asking?'

Alex laughed. 'I'm a ship's captain.'

Alex thought the store clerk was going to hurt himself from laughing so hard. 'Oh. Oh. I needed that. Thanks.'

'Any time,' Alex said dryly. When the clerk stopped laughing and was able to dry his eyes and take a deep breath, Alex added, 'Now about my order, if you don't mind. And make it cheap, if you please. I haven't much money.'

'Yes, sir. Let's see now. You say you'll be sleeping outside. And the nights are getting colder. You'll want two blankets, I think. I have some of the heavy wool blankets intended for the Indian trade. Those are seventy-five cents. Or if you really want to go on the cheap, I can give you some surplus army blankets. Only a quarter apiece. This lot isn't too ragged, but some of them have dried blood on them. I think they came out of a hospital somewhere.'

'I'll take the trade blankets then and live with the extra expense.'

'Right. Sulphur matches.' He looked

at Alex's stump, his lips pursed. 'You know, you'll need to cut wood if you want to cook and sleep warm. I have a Swedish bow saw that I think would do that for you. It's small and light enough that I think you could handle it. And a coat, of course. You need a good coat. I have a buffalo hide coat that's hell for heavy, but it'll keep you toasty warm right up until you freeze to death.'

Alex laughed. He liked this fellow, all the more so because the man did not pretend not to see the stump. Many people, most really, acted as if it weren't so. This man not only accepted it, he offered suggestions about overcoming the handicap. That was a refreshing departure from the usual.

'The coat is supposed to be five dollars, but what the hell. For a good customer like you . . . Can you manage three dollars?'

Alex thought about the coins he'd slipped inside the waistband of his trousers all the way back home in Georgia. He'd managed to come all this

way without resorting to them. But now
. . . He sighed and nodded.

'All right then. Now, let me see what
else I can think of that you'll need if
you want to go it afoot and alone up
there in the mountains.' The clerk
turned away and began rummaging
through the goods that were piled
willy-nilly through the rat's nest that his
store resembled.

3

I

'You get up and put some wood on the fire, will you? Personally, I'm not sure I want to get out from under these blankets until, oh, I don't know . . . April or May,' Alex mumbled.

The pup responded by squirming up beside Alex's chest until the tip of its moist nose protruded from beneath the edge of the blanket. It licked Alex's chin, the wet spot turning instantly frigid.

'Thank you so much,' Alex complained. But he was petting the pup while he did so. 'Not going to build that fire for me? Lazy cur. Just watch yourself, or it's the stew pot for you, bub.'

It was . . . what? September now? Maybe into October already. He had sort of lost track lately. But there was already a thin scurf of snow on the ground, and it felt cold enough to make a wooden Indian shiver.

A man down in Idaho Springs told him it sometimes got so cold up here that your spit would freeze before it hit the ground. After last night and this morning, Alex was almost willing to believe it.

'Lying here isn't going to get it done, is it? Alex said. He felt the pup's tail move in response. When he dragged the blankets aside, the pup bounded playfully out of the nest of warmth created by their combined body heat and went scampering about the camp on a mad tear.

'I wish I had that kind of enthusiasm for something as simple as getting up in the morning,' Alex said as he picked up a twig and began stirring the ashes of last night's dying fire.

He found a pocket of live coals, and the tip of the twig flared alight. Alex grunted and laid a handful of pine needles over the tiny flame, then some dry pine bark, and finally some of the wood chunks he'd cut the evening before. The pine needles were quickly consumed and were no longer necessary now that the blaze was rekindled. But they smelled so good on the crisp morning air that he added some more just for the pleasure of smelling them.

'What sounds good for breakfast, eh? How 'bout some left-over rice?'

The pup yipped and came rushing back to drop to its haunches and lean against Alex's side.

'Useless little beast,' Alex grumbled while he scratched the animal behind its ears. 'If only I could teach you to build a fire, hmm? Oh well. If this is the canyon I think it is, we'll be in Holihan in time for lunch.'

He scratched the pup some more, then scratched his own right armpit — it sometimes bothered him no small amount that there were so many places that he could not scratch, at least not without resorting to an implement of some sort — and he added more wood to the fire before he reached for his water can and poke of tea leaves.

There was a thin film of ice on the water he'd left in the can overnight.

That did not surprise him. The fact that the water was not frozen into a solid block did.

Alex yawned, then looked with trepidation upward to the sheer, gray stone walls that towered high on either side of this narrow defile.

'Helluva place for a seafaring man,' he said aloud.

The pup wagged its tail and pressed tighter against him.

II

Alex's feet hurt like fire — it was no consolation that this was the only form of warmth available at the moment — due to the boots he'd bought down in Denver City. He might have been better off buying used boots. They at least would have been broken in already. He would have done so, although for cost-saving purposes and not with forethought to the breaking-in process, except the two pairs of 'experienced' boots available were lace-up styles. He'd opted for the new pull-ons instead and now wished he hadn't.

At the other end of his frame he was being annoyed with mosquito-like persistence by a stray mustache hair that kept tickling his nose. One snip of his scissors would remove it. If only he had a mirror to search in. His only recourse was to grope blindly with cold-numbed fingers and try to snatch it free. So far, the only thing he'd accomplished was to make his upper lip sore and his nose run even more than it already had been. The hair was still in place, still tickling his nostril.

And now . . . now it seemed that he'd reached Holihan, Colorado Territory.

That was all he needed to top off his discomfort.

Holihan, Colorado Territory, was ugly.

Bad ugly.

Butt ugly.

Tie me down and gag me ugly.

Holihan, Colorado Territory, gave ugly new standards to which other uglies might aspire.

Holihan, Colorado Territory, was so bleak and colorless it looked like a magazine woodcut come to life.

It lay in the narrow, winding bottom of a canyon defile with massive granite walls on either side. Haphazard piles of weather-grayed timber, native stone, and muddy canvas served as buildings. A pall of acrid smoke hung above the roofs, blocking his view of everything between ground level and the highest levels of the canyon walls.

It might have been a blessing, he thought, if the smoke drifted even lower so as to obscure *everything* in this miserable, treeless, shades-of-gray insult to humanity.

Alex grunted softly and swiped a finger under his nose, both to try to smooth that damned hair out of the way and because his nose was running again.

'Come along then,' he said to the pup that was waddling happily along at his side. 'I think we're home, God help us.'

III

There wasn't much to choose from when it came to businesses where a man might step indoors and make inquiries. There were only half a dozen stores, half a dozen saloons, and roughly half a dozen boarding-houses. Alex could see only one normal house that looked like a one-family accommodation, but that one was grand enough to make up for the lack of others, it being tightly crafted of milled lumber instead of the rough timbers, rock, and canvas of the town's remaining buildings.

The house would not be considered either grand or a mansion back in Savannah. But here in Holihan it seemed both, if only in comparison, for it was painted as white as the snow that lay in drifts throughout the canyon and had a covered porch attached to its front and a row of scrawny poles that he guessed were intended to represent columns.

The house was quite noticeable as it was situated — literally - above the rest of the town, having been built 80 or 100 feet up the eastern slope of the canyon wall. Everything else lay strung along the rock-strewn bottom.

'That one's not for the likes of us,' Alex told the pup. It occurred to him after he said it that there was a time when he would have considered any such place appropriate for his visit. But that was some time ago now and very far away.

He entered instead the first mercantile he came to on the single street of Holihan, grateful to get inside again. A light snow was falling, and the temperature was bitter. He could only imagine what it would be like when serious winter set in.

'Mornin', mister.'

'Good morning, sir.' Alex removed the fur cap he'd gotten down in the city and brushed flakes of snow off his right shoulder. He couldn't reach his left so had to let the snow melt where it was.

'What can I do for you this morning?' the proprietor — the place was surely too small to employ a clerk in addition to its owner — asked with a welcoming smile.

'I'm looking for Bates Canyon.'

The fellow, a thin man with a receding hairline, blinked and gave him an odd look. 'You don't know where Bates is?'

'No, sir. They told me down in Denver City I should ask at Holihan. This is Holihan, is it not?'

'Oh, this is Holihan, all right. It's also Bates Canyon. Holihan is *in* Bates Canyon, d'you see. One's a town, t'other's a canyon. Friend, right this second you're standing in Bates Canyon.'

Alex hoped he didn't look as foolish as he felt. 'I didn't realize.'

The merchant shrugged. 'No harm done.'

'Would you know where I can find something, a real estate development I suppose, called Culbertson Filing?'

The man laughed. 'Mister, there's no such critter as a real estate anything hereabouts. There's just some mining claims and two active mines that grew out of the passle of claims that were filed back in the early days.'

'Then is there a town hall where records of these would be found?' Alex persisted.

'Not here, there isn't. Like I said, all we got these days is two working mines and what you see along this street. There used to be some more, but to tell you the truth, there wasn't all that much more, even when the place boomed. Bates never has been big pay. Not enough to put in a mill or anything like that. They dig the ore here an' haul it down to Golden for processing. We got, I dunno, three or maybe four hundred folks here. Most of them work in Henry Holihan's Big H mine. Then there's Ken O'Reilly's mine called the Irish Rover. And us merchants. That about covers it.'

'I see.'

'You might find some records up at the county seat. That's at Redear.'

'Red Ear?'

'Yes, but it's spelled together into one word.'

'I didn't come through any place called Redear.'

'You came up from Denver City, so of course you didn't. Redear is up the pass ten, twelve miles or so. Just past Rattlesnake Holler.' The man grinned. 'Don't let the name make you nervous. It's a joke, you see. Rattlers don't live at that elevation. There's some live lower and a variety that lives up higher, but there's no rattlers right at that level. Which is why somebody said if you see a rattlesnake, holler. But don't ask me how in tarnation Redear ever got its name, for I have no idea about that.

Thinking of names, friend, that's a fine-looking puppy that's peeing on my floor. What's his name?'

Alex looked around, and just as the man said, the pup was contentedly squatting in the warmth of the store, dribbling pee into a puddle on the crushed stone floor. 'Mister, I'm sorry; I'll clean it up.'

'Oh, don't worry about it. It'll seep in and go away. What'd you say his name is?'

Alex opened his mouth, but for an awkward moment, nothing came out. He'd never bothered to name the little dog. 'Bell,' he said quickly, thinking about his lost ship the *Savannah Belle.*

'Belle is a girl's name. That's a boy dog.'

'Don't tell him that, please. He doesn't know the difference.'

The gent laughed. 'All right then. You got me.'

'Sir, I thank you for your help. I wish I could afford to buy something from you, but right now . . . '

'Next time,' the merchant said cheerfully.

'Thank you, sir.' Alex pulled his cap back on and tugged on Bell's twine leash. 'Come along, Bell. Now that you've disgraced the both of us.'

They went back outside. It was bitterly cold, but the snow had stopped falling. Alex glanced at the steep slopes and precipitous walls that hung over the narrow canyon, but there was nothing visible to tell him just what portion of this tiny corner of the world was his.

He started walking back the way they'd just come.

IV

Redear was larger than Holihan but no more prosperous, at least in appearance. Ox, mule, and horse teams trudged through, creating an atmosphere of commerce that was not borne out by the shabbiness of the few buildings. The bulk of that traffic seemed to be coming from somewhere else and en route to somewhere else as well, with Reader being merely a spot in the middle that had to be passed through in order to get from start to stop.

Alex led the pup along the side of the road, concerned lest the inquisitive thing would stray beneath the wheels of one of the massive wagons that rumbled and clattered along the road that linked Denver City and the plains with whatever lay even higher into the snow-capped mountains.

For a country that didn't look like much, there was a powerful amount of traffic going up and down. The up-bound wagons were loaded with bags and bales and bundles carrying what appeared to be any and every manner of produce and product. The downhill traffic consisted almost exclusively of mounds of broken rock.

It seemed foolish to pay to transport pieces of shattered stone. Until Alex recalled that yesterday that fellow back in Holihan said something about the mines in Bates Canyon having to freight their ore down to . . . he tried to remember. It hadn't been Denver City the man mentioned. Golden. That was it. The ore was taken down to a mill in Golden, which he remembered was far down the pass, almost to the plains, but was indeed much closer than Denver City.

Alex paused to pick up a fist-sized chunk of the gray, slightly shiny stone that had fallen off one of the countless wagons. He'd never seen mineral ore before. And looking at it now, he had to conclude that gold — if indeed that was what this ore contained — was not impressive in its native state.

The stone was a mottled gray, its surface made shiny and reflective by tiny flecks of . . . he held it up within a few inches of his eyes so as to see better and peered at the rock closely . . . mica? It looked like minute bits of mica that were contained within the rock, those being the cause of the shining surface when they caught and reflected the light.

There was also some pebbling of other textures and colors. A little intrusion of pale quartz, he suspected. Flecks of some copper-colored something that he could not pretend to identify. Bits of blue and even green.

But gold? Not a trace of it. There was nothing in or on the ore chunk in Alex's hand that looked remotely gold-like to him.

It was probably, he concluded, a very good thing that he did not intend to take up prospecting, for he would have no idea what a prospector ought to look for. It was all just rock to him.

And apparently of small value in this unprocessed — whatever that consisted of — condition. The roadway was liberally strewn with the stuff, and no one paid the least attention to any of it. Had it been valuable, someone would surely have engaged themselves in recovering it. But then, judging by the many wagons traveling downhill with ton upon ton of the ore, there was indeed value to be found if the quantities were great enough.

'Not that you and I have to care about that,' Alex muttered to the pup, which cocked its head and twitched one ear when he spoke. 'Come along then.'

V

The Canton County courthouse was as unprepossessing as everything else in Reader. It was a single-story log structure with a shake roof and a large sign to announce its function. Alex judged the dimensions at no more than ten by twenty, large for a log building but decidedly on the small side when compared with other courthouses he'd seen.

Inside there was but one room cluttered with desks and shelving and filing cabinets. There was nothing that looked remotely like a courtroom, and only three people were working, although there were desks enough to

120

accommodate perhaps a dozen. Two men were standing beside one of the desks, presumably engaged in some form of official business.

'Who would I see about land plots?' Alex asked the nearer of the two unoccupied clerks.

'That would be Jim.' The fellow nodded to the other free clerk. He raised his voice a little. 'Hey! Jimbo. Somebody here to see you.'

The clerk smiled and motioned Alex to join him. 'Have a seat, mister. Tell me what I can do for you.'

Alex sat gratefully. It had been some time since he'd last been able to enjoy a piece of actual furniture. The pup sat also, tucking itself tight against his leg. 'I need to find a plot in Bates Canyon,' he said.

'It's plotted and recorded land, you say?' The clerk sounded skeptical. 'There isn't much filed down there. Not much need for it, you see. They had a brief boom, but there were only two workable veins discovered. Nobody ever surveyed the placer claims. Those were all worked out and useless by the time anyone gave thought to organizing. Are you sure it's Bates Canyon you're thinking of?'

'Oh yes. The plot is described as Culbertson Filing Number Eight.'

'Culbertson! Oh my. That would be on Henry Holihan's side of the canyon. On the east side, that is. Mr Holihan owns all that side of the canyon. It's where his Big H mine is, you see. A gentleman named O'Reilly owns most of the west side. That was recorded as the Jonas Filing. All the parcels in both filings have recorded ownership, of course. There aren't any open to preemption, if that's what you had in mind, sir.'

'I see. And this plot in the Culbertson Filing, you say that would be held by this Mr Holihan?'

'Yes, sir. He holds that entire wall of the canyon.'

Alex looked at the thick, canvas-bound ledgers stacked on sturdy shelving nearby. He was about to challenge the clerk's contention that Henry Holihan owned every parcel when the fellow added, 'If a man could get his hands on a piece of Culbertson, he would be a very rich man, I would think. Or a dead one.'

'Pardon me? Dead, you say?'

'Claim jumping is something we take very seriously here, sir. Very seriously. Hanging is the most likely outcome.'

'Gracious. That is serious indeed.'

'Yes, sir. Not that we've had any such occurrences lately. It has been, oh, probably three years since anyone was hanged here. And that was mostly because they were rebel sympathizers. They probably would have gotten off with a flogging and banishment if they'd been Unionists.' The clerk's smile was bland and quite matter-of-fact.

He'd thought about suicide before. Perhaps trying to claim that which was rightfully his could be regarded as a form of it. Alex thought about the simple, much-handled piece of paper that lay in the bottom of his haversack and decided against making any public claim to the parcel. At least for right now. 'Thank you, sir. Thank you very much for your help.'

'Any time, friend. That's what we're here for, you know.'

'Come along, Spot.' He'd decided he couldn't give the scrapper a girlie name. Spot seemed as good a name as any. He tugged at the leash to get the little dog to its feet, then gathered the twine onto the handhold of his crutch, and went out into the crisp, cold mountain afternoon.

Perhaps, he thought, coming here hadn't been such a good idea after all.

VI

Finding shelter in Redear was not a problem. There were four or five abandoned shanties to choose from. Alex picked one with a fireplace and spread his blanket close to it. Whoever built the place for some reason hadn't included a damper in the chimney, so most of the heat from his fire escaped uselessly upward, but even so, there was enough warmth to make the effort worthwhile. And the warm, occasionally squirming pup snuggled tight against him underneath the blanket helped, too.

Alex was comfortable enough. But he lay awake for a long time thinking. Mostly worrying.

The land that had been his brother's was occupied now by another. And from it, apparently, this Henry Holihan had become quite wealthy.

A man tends to protect his sources of income. All the more so if they are significant.

And the courthouse clerk's warning had been both explicit and unnerving. Documents are proof, but they are subject to challenge in a court of law. Alex had no way to know if the young men who conveyed the deed to Donald were alive now. So many of the South's finest did not survive to see the destruction wrought by their foes. He might well someday need their testimony as to the validity of the deed.

But first, of course, he had to make sure the deed remained in his possession.

Continuing to carry it loose in the bottom of his haversack suddenly seemed a dangerously lax practice. He'd traveled across half a continent without having to give thought to the security of his possessions.

Now he did.

He lay awake for a long time worrying about what to do.

At length, he grunted with satisfaction and patted the dog's ribs. 'In the morning,' he said aloud. 'We'll take care of it in the morning.'

The pup wagged its tail and idly licked Alex's stump.

Both man and dog slept soundly once his decision was reached.

'I'd like an envelope, please. And I'll need a stamp. Oh, and a pencil, too.'

'That will be six cents. Anything else, mister? Some paper maybe?'

'No, these will do just fine, thank you.'

Alex took his purchases outside. The morning was cold and clear, the recent clouds leaving only wind-scattered drifts and riffles of snow. He sat on the edge of the wooden sidewalk, and the pup whined a little as it pressed close to his ankle. 'I know. I'm hungry, too. We'll eat as soon as I'm done here.'

Out in the street, wagons rumbled past in a nearly constant flow, despite the early hour.

Alex peered balefully at the pencil he'd just purchased. It was a perfectly ordinary pencil. Cylindrical lead center. Thin wooden slab sides. Perfectly normal. And of course, being new, it had no point. The lead core was fully contained by the wooden sheathing. He needed . . . he needed his right hand was what he needed, dammit.

He felt a sense of frustration as he realized the difficulty that lay ahead of him with as simple a task as sharpening this pencil.

Dammit anyway!

Still, whining about it would do nothing to get the job done. Not any more than the pup's whining could make breakfast suddenly appear. It would be up to Alex to provide for both needs.

With a sigh, he slipped the haversack off his shoulder. The scissors given so long ago by Dr Fredericks were always packed on top of everything else, for he needed them daily. Their uses were endless. And this time . . .

His frustration built, however, even when he had the scissors in hand.

He had them in hand, all right. But he also needed to hold the pencil while he tried to pinch and slice with the cutting edge of the scissors. And scissors are *not* designed for this sort of work.

He tried sitting on the pencil and gnawing at the tip with the scissors, but that accomplished nothing except to splinter the pencil end. And barely even that, for he could not hold the pencil firmly in that manner, and it kept sliding away from the bite of the scissor jaws. Worse, the scissors would not properly grip an object as thick as a pencil, and he was afraid if he applied too much pressure, he would damage the scissors. And he depended on those. He could not imagine trying to get along without them.

He tried capturing the pencil between his ribs and his upper arm, but that was little better than sitting on it had been.

He tried stepping on it with the end of the pencil hanging over the side of the boards. That did hold the pencil steadier, but it did nothing to make the scissors grip or cut any better.

He tried chewing the pencil end, but the only thing he seemed to be accomplishing was to make the wood wet and get splinters and the sharp flavor of lead and cedar and paint in his mouth.

'Sir?'

He looked up. A lady stood behind him. Not a woman. A lady. The real thing. She was young. She was pretty. She was handsomely dressed in a cape and muff and ridiculously small — but entirely fashionable — fur hat.

'May I help you with that, sir?'

Alex's first impulse was to refuse. He did not want this young woman's pity.

But he did need the damned pencil sharpened.

'Yes, miss. That would be very kind of you.'

She bent down and plucked the pencil from beneath his arm — what of it remained, that is — and smiled. 'I won't be a moment.'

She disappeared inside the store where Alex had done his shopping, and true to her word emerged a few moments later with a blunt but fully exposed point on his pencil. 'There you are, sir.' Her smile was dazzling.

'Thank you, miss.'

'But of course.' She nodded politely, gathered her skirts, and swept off up the street.

It hadn't occurred to Alex that he could walk back inside the store and ask the man there to sharpen the damned pencil for him. He felt foolish. But looking at the back of the young woman as she walked away, swaying so prettily, he also felt . . . He shook himself. *Better not to open that can of worms*, he warned himself sternly. *No point in a cripple having thoughts about attractive girls. Not the sort of thoughts that a whole man would want to have, anyway.*

Glumly, he put such thoughts away and with more determination than skill proceeded to address the envelope to himself at . . . he spent a few moments deciding . . . at General Delivery, Idaho Springs, C.T.

The deed to Culbertson Filing No. 8 should be secure enough in a postal bin down there.

'All right then, small stuff,' he said when he was done. 'Let's go post this and then see what we can do about breakfast.'

The pup wagged its tail and followed eagerly.

VIII

He couldn't keep on indulging himself like this. He knew that before he did it. But he'd done it anyway. He'd gone into a restaurant and paid for a meal. Twenty cents. It probably should have been more. The waiter saw him slipping bits of meat and bread to the pup. Instead of making Alex pay extra, the man brought out some scraps from the kitchen and set them down for the pup. It was nice of him, Alex thought. Mighty nice. That bummer knew what he was talking about.

Alex stretched hugely, then leaned down to give the pup a scratch behind its ears. This would have to be their last store-bought meal for a while, he realized. After paying for his coat and blanket and things, he was down to a scant handful of coins in his pocket and one last double eagle still hidden inside the waistband of his trousers.

He had enough food to last for perhaps two weeks. Probably less. After that . . . He had no idea how he would get along after that. He needed to find work. If there was any work that a one-armed man could do in these mountains.

Still, right now things were not all that bad. He had a full belly. He could go back to that abandoned shack and sleep warm there tonight, then tomorrow head down to Holihan and . . . well, he'd just have to see about his next step when he got there. Hire a lawyer, maybe. That would be logical. He would see about all that when the time came.

'Come along, dog. Let's go make a fire and get warm.'

The camp that Alex presumed to be Rattlesnake Hollow looked like more of an ambition than an actuality. It consisted of three small buildings dug into the hillside where the hollow opened onto the pass where the road lay. The dug-out portions of the shacks were rather crudely augmented with native stone and warped aspen logs. They looked ancient, but Alex had already learned that was no indicator in this bleak, rocky country that had been prospected and inhabited for only a handful of years.

Smoke showed from the chimneys of two of the dug-outs, The third looked lifeless. No smoke drifted above it, and despite the chill that remained in the late-morning air, there was no door nor so much as a blanket or deerskin to block the air.

Yet it was from this cabin that two men emerged when Alex approached the tiny settlement on his way back to Holihan.

'Hello.' He nodded to the pair and gave them a smile.

Neither of the men smiled back at him.

Alex turned his attention away from them and walked on by. If they did not care to be friendly, that was their problem not his.

He heard footsteps close behind him, the sound of boot soles crunching on the gravel that covered the hard-packed earth on both sides of the creek that over time had carved this pass linking Denver City with the gold fields. He heard the footsteps very close by, and then the pup yelped as if in terror.

Alex started to turn, only to be interrupted by a loud, booming, drum-like sound. The back of his head went numb, his vision faded, and in his last moments of consciousness, he was aware that the sound was more felt than heard as one of the unfriendly men bashed him over the head.

Alex blinked, rather vaguely aware that he could feel the sharp, annoying prickle of gravel gouging into his cheek and chin and nose, even though he did not remember falling.

He began to hear more sounds of impact and grunts of exertion, but he did not actually feel the boots that were thudding into his body, and very soon he felt and heard nothing at all.

4

I

Damned wagon was bumping and bouncing, and every tiny jolt hurt something awful. Alex felt like his head was stuffed with cotton. His ribs and head and arms hurt like hell. And he knew that it would have been worse except for the fog that drifted through him.

He knew, though, what had happened. More or less. Up to a point. Those men beat him. For no reason at all, they waylaid him and beat . . . robbed him? He hoped not. He had little enough. He did not want to lose that little.

Now, he had no idea where he was. He seemed to be lying in a wagon. All right, he *knew* he was in a wagon. He could hear and feel that much. He did not know whose wagon. Or where it was going. He wished it would soon arrive, whatever the destination. The jolting of the unsprung vehicle was hard to bear.

As if by magical command, he thought the desire and at once the wagon came to a stop. 'Whoa. Whoa there.' He could hear the stamping of hoofs on hard ground and now that the pain of the movement was gone, he became aware of the feel of snow on his face. He was cold. But only his face. The rest of him, he discovered now that he paid attention to it, was covered with a thick blanket.

He tried to pull the blanket higher under his chin but for some reason could not get a grip on the darn thing. He tried and tried and . . .

Oh, God! A hot flush of shame rushed through him as he suddenly remembered. Without thinking about it, he'd reached to tug the edge of the blanket with his right hand. Years of habit had overcome months of newly enforced acceptance, and he'd acted spontaneously, pawing uselessly with his stump when he'd quite honestly thought he was grabbing at the hem of the blanket.

The knowledge served to waken him, driving away some of the mist that clouded his mind and sharpening his senses.

He heard the unseen and unknown teamster climb down from the driving box. Heard small grunts both human and animal. Heard the clink of metal on metal and the dull thump of a hitch weight being dropped onto the ground. Heard a strange voice call out, 'Hey! Jack. I got some cargo here I don't need. Found some guy all beat to hell and left in the road. D'you want him? I damn sure don't.'

The announcement brought a stir of voices in response, some sympathetic and some merely annoyed.

At length, several bearded faces appeared over the side of the lightly loaded wagon to peer inside. Hands reached for him. Picked him up.

The handling reawakened Alex's pain, and he thought he screamed once before passing out from the agony of being picked up and moved.

II

'Oh, my God. I know this man!'

'You know a bummer like this, Miss Beth?'

'Well, I don't exactly *know* him. But I spoke with him just yesterday. I helped him . . . never mind about that. And he didn't look so shabby and disheveled yesterday, Toby. He looked like a perfectly nice person. Except for, well, you know.'

'I suppose it's the beating that makes him look so bad. Not that it makes any difference now.'

'What do you mean by that, Toby?'

'He's gonna die, Miss Beth. Look at him. He won't last out the day.'

'I can't believe that, Toby. I won't

believe it. That's all. I simply will *not* accept any such thing.' There was a pause during which Alex heard nothing, then, 'Oh, don't give me that look. You know good and well. When my mind is made up about something, that is the end of it. And my mind is made up. I am going to take care of this poor man, Toby. I am.'

'Miss Beth, I — '

'No. Don't say it. I don't want to hear it. Would you be so good, please, as to tell Charles that I need him? I want the carriage brought around. He's to park it as close to the sidewalk as he can get. And find some men to help me carry him, would you, please?'

'Miss Beth, you can't do anything for him. He's gonna die. If you put him in your rig, you'll just get blood all over the upholstery for no purpose.' There was another pause. 'All right, ma'am.' The male voice sighed. 'At least let me spread something over the floor so's he won't muss things up so bad.'

'The seat, Toby. We shall place him

onto the seat. And he will *not* die. I shan't permit it, you see.'

'Yes'm. Whatever you say.'

Alex slipped out of consciousness again, welcoming the relief from pain that came with the dark curtain that lay so softly upon him.

III

'Who are you?' The voice was dry and cracked and unfamiliar. And it was his own voice. It had been . . . he didn't know how long it was since he was last able to speak. Did not know how long he'd been unconscious.

But he was still alive. He was certain of that, damn those men. They may have tried, but they hadn't killed him.

'Who are you?' he repeated.

'I be Hazy.' The way she said it made it clear that she was giving her name, not a description. She was very fast and very black. She was seated in a rocking chair beside his bed, doing some sort of needlework in her lap.

'Is . . . where am I, Hazy?'

'This Miz Beth O'Reilly's town home, mistuh.'

'Town home?'

'Tha's right. Town. We in Denver. Miz Beth and Mistuh Ken, they got homes up on de mountain an' down here, too.' She smiled. 'They right rich folk, mistuh. Got homes, carriages, all that.' The smile became bigger. 'An' they got me as been tendin' you since Miz Beth brought you down heah. What yo name, mistuh? What name you go by?'

'Alex,' he told her. 'Is that a pitcher of water I see over there? Could I have some, please? I feel dry as a bone.'

'Bone is 'bout all they is to you now, too, Mistuh Alex. You been passed out pret' near a week now. No wonder you got you a thirst.' While she spoke, she was busy pouring water into a glass, lifting his shoulders off the pillow, holding the glass to his lips.

'God, that tastes good,' he said as the

cool, soothing water flooded his mouth and trickled down his parched throat.

'I glad it taste good t' you, Mistuh Alex, but don't you be takin' the Lord's name in vain like that no more. It ain't fittin' to do that.'

'Sorry.' It was an admonition he'd heard plenty in his youth. But not since he went to sea. Certainly not since his mother died.

'You want more?'

'Yes, please.'

She lifted him up again. But only long enough to allow him another swallow. No more. 'That's 'nuff now, Mistuh Alex. Too much in yo stomach at once be bad for you. 'Sides, you got to save room. I'm gonna go down now an' fetch up some warm soup for yo belly. That make you feel better. Plenty better.'

'All right. Thank you.'

The roly-poly black woman stood, and he realized that she probably was bigger around than she was tall. He could not be sure from where he lay, but he suspected she would have to stand on a stool to tape out at five feet. She set the glass of water on the bedside table and left. He could hear her footsteps descending a staircase somewhere close by.

Alex tried to reach for the glass. With his right hand. Annoyed, he tucked the stump underneath the sheet that covered him and gave up on the water. He felt too weak to roll over and try to reach the table with his left hand.

IV

Chicken soup, Alex decided, was very likely the most perfect restorative known to mankind. Chicken soup, that is, and the milk and honey that Hazy also insisted he drink. 'You drink this now, Mistuh Alex. This recipe come right outa the Bible. It fix you right up.'

It did, too. Mostly. Two days of this regimen and he was feeling considerably better, able to sit up unassisted and employ the chamber pot without assistance. That was a relief. Having to accept help for something so intensely personal was more than merely embarrassing. He found the experience to be positively mortifying.

It would not have been quite so bad had there been a male attendant available, but Hazy was the only other person in residence at the O'Reilly town house at the moment. Or so she explained.

'My man Charles, he drives Miz Beth. She be up the mounteen now. She tell me to take good keer o' you till she get back though. An' that be what I'se doing.'

'You are indeed taking good care of me, Hazy. The best. Thanks.'

'You want some more milk an' honey, Mistuh Alex? Just a swallow or so?'

'Yes, please.' He was surprised to discover that the stuff actually tasted darn good. Excellent, in fact. He was not so sure about eating the locusts that were supposed to accompany milk and honey. Fortunately, Hazy did not attempt to serve him any bugs, locusts or otherwise.

Hazy hurried downstairs to mix another glass of it for him. It amazed Alex that she could remain so stout — fat, really — despite constantly dashing upstairs and down. He would have thought the exercise would peel away some of her bulk, but it did not. And she seemed quite comfortable just as she was.

He lay back against the mound of pillows she'd provided for him and closed his eyes.

Tomorrow, he thought. Tomorrow he would see if he could stand and walk a little without help.

But not today.

He was asleep again when Hazy returned with his milk and honey.

V

It felt like quite an accomplishment. He went downstairs for breakfast. That sounded like a simple thing perhaps, but it was not. It took days of slow recovery before he thought he was up to it, and even after that, Hazy insisted on helping him, half carrying him every step of the way. That was not really all that difficult for her because as little as she was — at least as to height — she fit beneath his armpit like a warm, chubby crutch.

Once downstairs, Alex found that it did feel marvelous to be able to sit in a proper chair, at a proper table, and enjoy a proper meal, and never mind the expense in terms of pain and weariness that so simple a journey caused. He was still far from healed.

Hazy served him enough food to feed a family of six and stood nearby ready to bring more if he should request it.

'This is good, Hazy. Thanks.' He took a bite of crisp, fried potatoes dripping with grease and salt. They were wonderful. 'When will your mistress be home?'

'Oh, she don' tell me nothing,

Mistuh Alex. She come an' she go, but she never say when.'

'I owe her my life.' He smiled. 'Owe you, too, for that matter. Don't think I don't know it.'

'I just doing the Christian thing, suh. And doin' what I been tole to do.'

'You've done much more than you had to, Hazy. I'd like to reward you.' He laughed. 'If I ever have anything to reward you with. Do you know what became of my things?'

He'd awakened wearing a nightshirt and had access to a constant supply of fresh, clean nightshirts, carpet slippers, and toilet items like tooth powder and a hard-bristled toothbrush. He'd asked for and received a hairbrush and some scissors to trim his beard and mustache. But he hadn't seen his own clothing since he found himself in this house.

'I washed an' mended them clothes you was wearing, Mistuh Alex. Cleaned up yo boots an' coat an' the like. They all put away. I can bring them to yo room later if'n you like.'

'What about my knapsack, Hazy? Oh, my! I just now . . . What about my dog? Where is my dog, Hazy?'

'Mistuh Alex, I don' know nothing 'bout no sack nor no dog. I ain't seen nothing o' them. Jus' you an' the things you was wearing.'

Now that he was aware of it, the loss — especially the loss of the pup — ruined the joy of being able to take his meal downstairs. Alex hadn't realized how attached he'd become to that little dog until now that it was gone.

VI

He was still brooding about losing the dog — but moving and feeling considerably better — a week later when at dinner Hazy announced that 'Miz Beth, she be home t'morra sometime. She send down a note. Tell me have ever'thing ready.'

Alex could not imagine anything extra needing to be done in preparation. Hazy kept the O'Reillys' town house immaculate every day already. 'I'll be pleased to meet her.'

'She say she already know you, Mistuh Alex. Be'n't that so?' she asked from her station behind and slightly to the left of his chair.

'If she says so. I remember a young woman helping me with a small task when I was in Redear, but I wouldn't claim that I know her. To tell you the truth, Hazy, I'm not sure I even remember what she looks like.' Lately, Alex had grown accustomed — more or less — to speaking to someone he could not see and hearing Hazy's responses from behind. He still did not care for the detachment though and turned now in his chair to face her.

The round little black woman grinned. 'You be knowing her when you sees her, Mistuh Alex. Just you wait an' see if I lie to you.'

'I'll take your word for that. And I'd

take another pork chop if you'd hand me that platter yonder.'

Hazy hurried to the table so she could comply, selecting a chop with plenty of crisply fried, tasty fat on it, and carefully cutting the tender meat into bite-sized pieces for him before she stepped back again.

Tomorrow, Alex reflected as he slowly chewed. He only wished there was something he could do to repay the O'Reillys' kindnesses.

He would just have to think of something.

VII

Hazy was right. He recognized her. Instantly. Beth O'Reilly was a vision of beauty. A classic portrait in the flesh. A Grecian frieze come to life. She fair took his breath away. And he needed no introduction to remember this exquisite creature who had twice now come to his rescue when he needed something, once with as mundane a need as a sharpened pencil and now . . . now with his very life.

Alex was seated outdoors on the veranda taking the sun when a carriage came up the street at a spanking, high-stepping trot. It was a glorious day, not nearly so cold down here in the city, although to the west he could see snow on the mountain slopes. In the clear, crisp air, the mountains appeared close enough to touch.

He only wished Mrs O'Reilly were close enough to touch. And that she would welcome his advance to . . . Stop! Any such thing as that was lost to him now. He was no longer a whole man. No woman would look at him now. It was time he put such yearnings, even the thought of them, clearly and permanently out of mind.

But, oh, she was lovely today.

The one time he remembered seeing her before, she'd been bundled inside a cocoon of cape and hat and muff. Today, in this excellent weather, she sat, chin high and proud, on the seat of a phaeton. The leather top was folded back to allow her also to enjoy the sun's warmth on this lovely day. A Negro of indeterminate age but exceptional size perched on the high driving seat to handle the lines, and Alex could see the back of another head, this passenger a white man, who rode not beside Mrs O'Reilly on the forward-facing seat but apparently crouched on a jump seat or robe bench at the front of the passenger compartment.

Alex's attention quite naturally enough was locked primarily on the lady.

She had gleaming black hair coifed in swirls and curls that framed a heart-shaped face with a pouting bow of ruby lips, small chin, round and dimpled cheeks, and the largest, greenest, deepest eyes Alex ever saw.

He saw all of this and was transfixed, even in the brief moments it took for the driver to wheel the phaeton past and into the drive leading to the rear of the house.

The phaeton came to a rocking halt beside the veranda, and the white man leaped out to help the lady down.

She was tall, Alex saw now. And slender. Her bustle and the fashionably tight body wrapping required to make her appear that she had no bosom made it impossible for him to assess her figure. Not that he had any right to do so.

'Madame,' he said, rising and making a leg before her, the elegance of the bow hampered by his inability to sweep his right arm as part of the motion, 'I am your devoted servant.'

VIII

'A ship's captain?' She began laughing, a full-bodied laughter coming from deep within and allowed to explode without any pretense at ladylike restraint. 'I think that is perfectly marvelous,' she exclaimed when she again had breath for words. 'A ship's captain. Imagine! And are you here seeking employment, Captain?'

Alex smiled. They were in the parlor, Beth O'Reilly seated as if royalty in a plush wingback chair; Alex and her employee, Toby Madison, arranged before her in positions and on furniture that clearly spelled out their subordination to the lady of the manor. Alex recognized this as a simple enough fact and took no resentment from it. He owed her that and considerably more.

'Not exactly,' he answered, still smiling.

'What does bring you so far from the sea, Captain?' she persisted.

Alex opened his mouth to explain this admittedly odd choice. Then, remembering the beating and the theft of all he owned, he changed his mind. After all, those events could well have been related to his admissions at the Canton Country courthouse. A clerk may have said something about his inquiry. Someone may have overheard while he was in the records office. After all, he'd felt a need to protect himself by hiding the deed certificate in the US Mail. It made no sense for him to become incautious now.

'I was hoping to find my fortune in your mountains,' he said. It was not untrue.

'Colorado is a land of dreams, Captain. And some riches also. Kenny and I would be the last to deny that opportunity exists here.'

'I did hear that you and your husband have done wonderfully well for yourselves here, Mrs O'Reilly. I'm happy for you.'

'Husband? Hardly. Kenny is my brother. He has a perfectly dutiful little wife, thank goodness, so I needn't worry over his welfare.'

'My apologies for the misunderstanding, Miss O'Reilly.'

She showed her dimples in his direction, then turned her pretty head and said, 'Toby, please see if Hazy has my tea ready.'

Madison stood. 'She's probably sneaked into the pantry with Charles. I'll go chase them out.'

'Do that, Toby. I'm thirsty. And tell her to bring some scones also.' She gave Alex another smile. 'The captain and I shall take tea now and become better acquainted.' The smile became positively dazzling in intensity. 'Shan't we?'

Tea and scones. And the company of a beautiful young woman. Why not? 'It will be my pleasure, miss.'

IX

Once the sun went down, it was too cold outside to retire to the veranda, so after supper, Beth O'Reilly led the way into the parlor. She curled like a contented cat beneath a warm robe while Toby built a fire in an ornate, nickel-plated stove, and Alex, at the lady's direction, poured white wine from a decanter. He served Beth, set a glass for Toby beside one of the chairs, and claimed for himself the chair best situated for viewing Beth O'Reilly's beauty.

'Toby,' Beth said when the gentleman in question finished with the fire and joined them, 'I think you should tell Captain Adamley what you related to me this afternoon.'

Madison gave her a slightly troubled look, glanced in Alex's direction, and then to the lady said, 'I shouldn't of said anything, Miz Beth. It's only a rumor, after all. I don't really know anything.'

'Even so,' Beth said firmly, 'I believe he has the right to hear this.'

'But it might be nothing, ma'am, it might be — '

'Toby!' Her voice remained low, but its tone was unmistakably firm.

'Yes, ma'am.' The hired man — Alex had no idea what function he served — turned to Alex. 'It's something I heard a couple days ago up in Holihan. You know the place?'

'Not well but . . . yes. I do.'

'Yeah, well, that's where Miz Beth an' Ken have their other house. And the mine, of course. They own the Irish Rover, see.'

Alex nodded.

'Get to the point, Toby,' Beth snapped.

Toby sighed. 'I really shouldn't ought to've said anything, Adamley. Probably not a thing to it. But one evening I was playing cards with some fellows. I happened t' overhear what some boys at another table were saying. Mind now, I wasn't listening in deliberately, an' I didn't hear everything that was said. It wasn't like that. But I couldn't help overhearing some of what they were saying, y'see. And it . . . one of them . . . they said something about being disappointed because they jumped some guy an' beat him up but didn't get whatever it was they were supposed to.

'That's about all of it. I never heard more, you understand. And I never gave any thought to you an' your situation at the time. On the way down here today, I was passing the time, talking with Miz Beth, and she's the one thinks mayhap there is a connection between what happened t' you and what I overheard up there in Holihan.'

'Tell him the rest, Toby.'

'It isn't . . . you got to understand, Mr Adamley, that I don't really know what those boys were talking about. But I did turn my head at one point and look at them. They seen me do that and shut up on the subject of beating and robbing. But when I looked at them, see, I couldn't help but notice they were all guards from the Big H mine. That's the mine owned by a fellow name of Henry Holihan. I recognized them from there. I don't exactly know them, but I've seen them around. It's a small town, after all, and if a fellow doesn't work one place, then he pretty much has to work at the other. And I knew good and well they weren't any of our boys.

'Anyway, like I said, I can't say for sure what their talk was about and shouldn't be saying anything to you at all, since all I have is doubts an' suspicions an' no real knowledge. I shouldn't ought to be pointing fingers at folks without knowing the truth, and wouldn't of said a word to you about this except Miz Beth insists. Just in case.'

'Did you lose anything of value when you were assaulted, Captain?' Beth asked in a voice filled with sympathy and gentle concern.

'Food. Blanket. Like that. Nothing of great value, if that is what you mean.'

'I am terribly relieved to hear that,' she said. 'And I want you to take Toby's comments as a warning. Is there anything you would like to tell us?' Her smile was dazzling. 'Anything you would like to tell *me*?'

He shook his head. 'No, miss. I think not.'

'As you wish, Captain. But please do keep in mind that I am here for you, if ever you need a friend or a confidante.'

'Thank you.' He took a sip of the white wine. It was a poor substitute for good brandy, and as wines go, he'd encountered better in the south of

France and in Spain, but it was acceptable apart from that. 'You are very kind.'

Toby excused himself and left the parlor without bothering to try the wine. He looked vaguely troubled, undoubtedly as a result of being asked to spread rumors.

'Now,' Beth said with a bright and chipper demeanor. 'Please tell me about yourself, Captain . . . May I call you Alex? . . . Please tell me everything about yourself. Everything.'

X

Alex lay snug beneath clean sheets and an eiderdown comforter. News that Miss Beth was on her way had galvanized Hazy into a frenzy of cleaning. Alex considered himself lucky that she hadn't insisted on coming after him with a scrub brush and pail. But he liked the smell and the feel of sun-dried, freshly ironed sheets and enjoyed the warmth that seeped up through the register from the coal-fired stoves downstairs.

It was late — he had no idea of the time but knew the hour would be small — but he was not able to sleep. He kept thinking about the conversation Toby Madison overheard in Holihan.

Disappointed that they hadn't gotten what they sought, were they? Well, it wasn't like he failed to consider the possibility of theft. After all, that was why he'd mailed the deed to himself.

Even so, it was one thing to consider that in the abstract, quite another to endure the pain and the humiliation of the beating and the robbery.

They'd left him for dead, and so they must have thought they had the deed in hand when they slunk away, taking his haversack with them. Cowardly sons of bitches! Couldn't even face a one-armed man.

There had been a time . . .

Ah. Enough! That was then. Things were different now. But the simple truth was that Alex was becoming angry.

How dare those backstabbing cowards do this? How dare they think they could so easily get away with it?

One arm or a dozen, he did not want them to go scot-free, damn them.

He would . . . He didn't know what he would do. Exactly.

But he would *not* simply lie about wallowing in self-pity while up on that mountain Henry Holihan's guards sat swilling beer and playing cards. Probably casting lots for his few possessions, he bitterly imagined. Like the Roman soldiers had done at the foot of the cross. Except Alex was not as meek and forgiving as that innocent victim had been.

Damn them anyway. He wondered if Madison knew the names of the men whose conversation he'd overheard or at least had a description of them.

Alex intended to find out at the earliest opportunity. That decided, he closed his eyes and this time had no difficulty falling into a deep and restful sleep.

XI

'What will you do with yourself now, Captain? Do you have any plans?' Beth asked a week and a half later. They were seated in the library after breakfast with copies of newspapers from Kansas City and New Orleans brought in yesterday's post and the latest edition of Denver's own *Rocky Mountain News* as well.

Alex had difficulty handling the pages of a newspaper, but Beth was courteous enough to allow him to manage on his own. He liked that about her. Liked as well the fact that she was a voracious reader with wide-ranging tastes. Her library was amply stocked, and he had enjoyed it thoroughly during his stay here.

A stay which he had to assume was coming to an end, considering the question she'd just now raised.

Not that he could complain. Hardly. The lady's generosity was exemplary, and he would forever be grateful to her for it.

He laid the folded pages of the *Picayune* in his lap and smiled now, trying to give an impression of unconcern as he responded, 'No specific plans, miss. But I do need to get on with my life. I'm recovered now, thanks to you, and I do not want to impose further on your kindness.' He laughed. 'I will have to ask Hazy to scout out my clothing, though. I've been in borrowed togs of one sort or another ever since I got here. If you would ask her to do that, I would appreciate it. And I appreciate all the more your generosity. I could never express to you — '

'Wait, Captain. Please. You misunderstand me,' she interrupted. 'I am not suggesting that you leave. Quite the contrary. Now that you are recovering, sir, I would take it as a great kindness if you would assist my brother and me.'

Alex was more than a little surprised. Whatever did she think a one-armed man could do? And the master of a sailing vessel at that! The nearest deep water was . . . what? . . . two thousand miles in either direction? The estimate was certainly close enough, even if not precise.

He had little choice, however, but to answer, 'Miss Beth, I would be honored to do anything for you that is within my power.'

'I've noticed you are an educated man, Captain. Sad to say, there are few enough men in the gold camps who can scratch their own names onto paper. You are intelligent, well read, in short, you are exactly the sort of man who would be an asset to us. Captain Adamley, would you consider accepting employment as office manager of the Irish Rover?'

'I . . . I don't know what to say, miss. You surprise me.'

'Fine.' She laughed, the sound of her voice delicate and sweet. 'I understand that. This is not something we've discussed before, although it is certainly a matter that has occupied my thoughts for the past few days. My question remains. Will you do this for us? For me?'

'For you, Miss Beth, I would do anything.' He meant that more sincerely than she likely understood, for the truth was that he was more than a little enamored of this elegant and beautiful young woman. And to now have an employment opportunity that would allow him to continue to see her in any capacity however base . . . 'I would be honored, miss, and once again find myself in your debt.' He rose, unheeding of the newspaper that fluttered to the floor, and bowed to her as gallantly as he could manage.

XII

At least his buffalo coat and fur hat had survived the ordeal of beating and robbery. Apparently, he'd still been wearing them when he was found, for they were among the clothing brought to him by Hazy, everything cleaned and mended and starched and ironed as well. Apart from his clothes, though, he had virtually nothing. The last of his father's gold coins had disappeared from his waistband along with everything else he'd owned.

Of the loss his greatest regret, oddly, was that of the scissors old Dr Fredericks gave him. He had come to depend on those scissors over the months since he lost the *Belle* . . . and somewhat more.

But then, loss seemed to be becoming the story of his life this past . . . How long had it been? Less than a year, now that he thought about it. Just short of a year. It was January when he made his last attempt to run the damn Yankee blockade. Now it was nearing the end of November. Rather a lot had changed in that time.

'Are you ready, Adamley?'

'I am, Mr Madison.'

'Come along then. We don't want to keep Miz Beth waiting.'

'No, of course not.' He followed Toby through the kitchen and outside, into the dry, biting cold and clear, brilliant sunshine of a late fall day in Colorado. The carriage, a closed rig this time, was waiting. Charles and Hazy disengaged from an embrace and whispered hurried goodbyes as the white men came outside. Charles opened the door for Toby and Alex to enter. Toby climbed in, but tiny, tubby Hazy stopped Alex with a tug on his empty sleeve.

'Mistuh Alex, they something I got to do.'

'What would that be, Hazy?'

'I foun' something when I wash yo pants, suh. I thought to keep it. Sho'ly I did. But I can't, suh. Can't feel good about it. It been worryin' at me ever since I found it. Here, suh. I'm awful sorry. I hope in your heart you can forgive me.'

She held out her hand, palm open to display a single coin of bright gold.

Alex smilingly lied, 'There it is. I thought I'd dropped that somewhere, and losing it distressed me because I wanted to give it to you as a thank-you for your kindness while I was healing.'

'But — '

'No 'buts'. You brought me back to health, Hazy. Words are not enough to express my gratitude.'

'Miz Beth, she — '

'I know she did, Hazy, and I shall do everything I can to repay her for that. But you are the one who did so much for me in this house.' He took her hand and curled the fingers back over her palm so as to trap the coin there. 'That is yours.'

'But, I — '

'Please.'

She bobbed her head and gave a little shuffle that was probably intended as a curtsy, then dropped the coin into an apron pocket before she ran inside to fetch a shovel of glowing red coals to stuff into the foot warmer inside the carriage.

Alex doubted the coals would last long, but their presence would be welcome for as long as they gave off heat.

He climbed inside the carriage and sat on the rear-facing bench as Toby indicated. As soon as Alex was settled, Charles drove around to the front of the house, where Beth would be picked up and helped inside.

This trip into the mountains promised to be a more comfortable one than the last Alex had taken.

He did miss that pup, though, damn them. Damn them.

5

I

As far as Alex could see, the Irish Rover had little need for an office manager. Everything seemed entirely in order already. Production, payroll, shipment, income, expense ... everything was accounted for and set down in a tidy, careful hand. Well, that was certainly about to change, he thought rather bitterly. He had practically no experience with left-handed writing and shuddered to think how these books would look now that they were under his inexpert care.

'Are you sure you want me to do this?' he protested.

'Quite, thank you. The position is yours, Captain. I have every confidence you will fill it handsomely.' She smiled. 'But then how could so handsome a man do otherwise?' She whirled abruptly, her skirts flying wide, and ran lightly up a steep staircase to another office that perched like an aerie atop the Irish Rover's administration building.

Alex was not at all sure he'd heard her correctly. Handsome? Hardly. Oh, there had been a time when he might have been considered so. But no longer.

He considered following her into the upstairs office, if only to pursue that last comment further.

As it turned out, there was no need. Beth came back down again after barely taking time enough to poke her nose inside the door at the top of the steps. A man, young and vigorous of appearance, followed close behind.

The man had black, curly hair and startlingly blue eyes over ruddy cheeks and a monstrously large mustache.

'Captain Adamley, may I present my brother Kenneth. Kenny, this is the gentleman I've been telling you about. Captain Adamley has agreed to run the office for us, dear. Won't it be wonderful to have that burden taken from us?'

Her smile was huge and lovely when she spoke, but Alex was not so sure about Ken O'Reilly's opinion. The owner of the Irish Rover nodded and extended his hand. But his expression seemed forced and in truth not entirely welcoming. 'My pleasure, Adamley.' The words were correct but held no warmth.

Alex took O'Reilly's right hand with his own left, the handshake as awkward for Alex as it seemed to be for O'Reilly although perhaps for different reasons. 'Your servant, sir.'

O'Reilly grunted.

Beth continued as chipper and chattery as a magpie. 'We've had a tiring trip, Captain, and tomorrow is Saturday. Why don't you rest over the weekend and begin afresh on Monday morning. Toby can show you to your quarters. Oh, and one more important thing I forgot to mention before. I've sent word to the mercantiles in Holihan that you are authorized to draw whatever personal items you may need. Your purchases will go on the company books, and you can reconcile them from your pay after the bills come in. Does that sound fair, Captain?'

'More than,' Alex agreed. 'Thank you very much.'

'Good.' Her smile was dazzling. 'Now, if you don't mind, Captain, I need to speak with my brother.'

'Of course, miss.' Alex bowed — he was becoming more comfortable with the gesture after having some practice at it — and both Beth and Kenneth O'Reilly returned to the upstairs office, leaving Alex below to go scout out Toby Madison and learn just where it was that he was expected to live.

II

They gave him a house of his own. Well, he supposed it would be considered a house. A hole had been dug perhaps six feet into the hillside — on the Irish Rover side of the canyon — and twelve or so feet wide. Side walls made of piled stone extented out from the hillside for another four or five feet. The front wall was also fashioned from unmortared stone. Wooden beams supported a sod roof. There was no chimney, but a rusting pipe showed where a stove once sat.

'I'll have some of the men bring a sheepherder stove in and tie it into the pipe,' Madison said. 'That will do you for the time being.'

'All right, thanks.'

'If you don't like this place, pick another. There's plenty to choose from. Just find one that's sitting empty. Only reason I thought of this one is that this stuff hasn't been taken off by somebody.' Toby gestured toward the interior where a rope-sprung bed was built into the back wall. A crude table and two stools were also present, and there were shelves pegged into the side wall to the left or south side of the house. There was even some tarnished and filthy tinware still stacked on the shelving.

'Whoever built this left in a hurry,' Alex observed.

Madison shrugged. 'Fella hears about a bonanza, he doesn't want anything slowing him down. He mostly grabs what he can carry on his back and heads out in a high hurry. Happens all the time. Even . . . hell, especially . . . among men who have good jobs underground. They see all that ore coming out o' the ground, and they want it to be their ore and have other guys working underground for them. So they grab their things and go. We lose thirty, forty percent of the work force every time there's news of a new strike. Doesn't matter how far away it is or whether it's proved. Word spreads, and the men rush to make their own finds, wherever the new place is.'

'But you haven't done that.'

Madison shook his head. 'Not me. I draw good pay. Got nobody but myself to spend it on. I'm satisfied here.'

'You've been with the O'Reillys for a long time, have you?'

'Since the start, practically.' He snorted. 'I was here when it was still called Bates. I filed a claim here myself just a few roads north of where Ken hit his vein. He knew he had his strike, and by then I knew that I didn't an' never would on that claim. Ken offered me work, and I took it. Helped him break rock to make that very first drift, him and me and half a dozen other fellows swinging hammers and turning drills. Ken did his own powder work then, too. He knows what he's doing underground, for he's swung a hammer and lit a fuse many and many a time. He doesn't do the work now, of course. But he keeps an eye on things. He knows what's happening in the Rover.'

'You like him,' Alex prompted.

'I do. Ken's tough and he's fair and he's always been straight and honest with me. Even bought my claim. He didn't have to do that. I would've given it to him if he asked, and he knew that.

But he didn't take advantage. He paid me way more than it was worth. The mechanical shop sits on it now.'

Alex tried to remember the names of the north Georgia boys who'd come here hoping to make their fortunes, only to hurry home when war came and eventually sign their deed over to Donald. He couldn't. But then that had been his brother's investment, not his. He remembered meeting the gold seekers, but their names and faces were but fuzzy partial recollections after all this time. He had thought to ask Madison if he'd known them, having been in the canyon since those early days. Another time perhaps.

'I forgot to tell you,' Madison was saying now, 'you can take your meals at Gerald Benton's boardinghouse.' Toby stepped just outside the door and pointed. 'It's that one down there. You see where I mean?'

Alex nodded. The large building sat close to the bottom of the slope at the near edge of what passed for a down.

'Just tell them who you are. They'll bill the company for your keep. I don't remember what the regular mealtimes are, but there's a list posted inside. And the Rover works round the clock, seven days a week. If you want a snack or something, you can get it in the kitchen there any time, day or night. That's part of their agreement with the company. Ken takes care of his people.'

'So I gather. Thanks.'

'You want any help bringing stuff up from the stores? You'll need blankets, clothes . . . stuff.'

'No, I can handle that, thank you.'

'All right then. I'll have someone fetch that stove in and have them lay in some coal, too. What we mostly do, those who live by ourselves, is let our fires die out while we're working, then carry a shovel of coals down from the office stove so we can light our own fires again come evening. Is that all right, or should I have somebody make your fire for you every night?'

'I can manage it myself, thanks.'

'All right then. Now, if you'll excuse me, Captain, there's things I have to take care of.'

'Yes. And thank you. You've been a wonderful help.'

Madison gave him a look that Alex could not interpret, then turned and hurried back up the canyon side toward the mine.

It was not until the man was well out of hearing that a question occurred to Alex. If the company contracted with the boardinghouses and intended him to eat in one of them, why hadn't they asked him to room there also? It would have seemed easier.

Perhaps it was a gesture of consideration for his privacy. Or it simply may not have occurred to whoever it was who directed all these helpful arrangements.

Not that it mattered.

Alex went back inside his new home so he could get a better idea of what little he had in there and how much he needed to buy down in the town.

III

It was too late for lunch and too early for dinner, and Alex wasn't all that hungry anyway, so he went down a winding path into the canyon bottom where the town was. From these new quarters he would walk uphill to work, downhill to eat or shop.

His first stop was the same store where he'd gotten directions before on his one brief visit to Holihan. He hadn't been able to afford anything there at that time. Now it seemed only fair to give this fellow his trade. The proprietor remembered him.

'Where's your pup?'

'I lost him.'

'That's a shame.'

'Yes, it is.' Alex did not want to elaborate on just how he'd lost the pup. He supposed it had wandered in the vicinity of Rattlesnake Holler until either somebody took it up as a stray or a bear or bobcat or owl had it for breakfast. He hoped somebody found it and took it in.

'Come looking for directions again, have you?' the storekeeper asked. But he was smiling when he said it.

'No, sir, this time I came to buy. I need to outfit myself pretty thoroughly and charge it all to the Irish Rover.'

'You the fellow Toby Madison said to look out for?'

'I expect that I am.'

'In that case, friend, let's be fitting you out with two of everything I've got. Ken O'Reilly's money spends just fine. So, what can I do for you?'

He thought about trying to skimp by on as little as possible. Then remembered that what he bought here was not a gift from the O'Reillys but an advance against salary. He would earn every bit of it.

So there was quite a lot this nice gentleman could do for him.

'I'll need a suit,' Alex said promptly. 'Off the rack will be acceptable for the time being. Smallclothes, boiled shirt, collars, and necktie. One of those pre-tied things that have hooks and eyes

185

to hold them together.' He smiled. 'I don't think I could manage to tie one properly these days. Sleeve garter, of course.' The smile turned into a grin. 'I only need one of those, I think. And . . . let me see . . . I'm open to suggestion.'

It occurred to him afterward that his adjustment to the damn Yankee disfigurement was easier now that he had employment and a sense of being able to earn his own way in the world.

That, it seemed, had been taken from him along with the arm. Now, with the self-respect accorded by employment, things looked brighter to him than they had since the day he lost the *Belle*.

Alex completed his shopping — he very nearly did buy two of everything in the place, or so it felt at the time — and accepted the proprietor's suggestion that he have the purchases delivered. It would have taken him a half dozen trips, perhaps a dozen, for Alex to carry it all himself.

'Will you please put the delivery

boy's pay onto my bill, too?' Alex asked. 'I don't have a cent of cash to my name right now.'

'Easily done,' the gentleman assured him. 'While I'm about it, would you like me to add five or ten dollars for you to put into your pocket? I wouldn't mind, and I doubt the people in the Irish Rover office will know the difference. I can hide it as . . . I don't know . . . I'll think of something.'

Alex laughed. 'I think that will be approved in the company accounts. In fact, I'm sure of it.' He himself, after all, would be the one to approve the payment.

'Ten dollars then?'

'Please.'

It was, he decided, a distinct pleasure doing business with this man.

IV

A job, a place to sleep, food in the larder, clothes to wear, and money in his pocket . . . it felt almighty good to have these things again. They made him feel almost normal. Almost.

Alex signed for his purchases, awkwardly perhaps, but sign he did, and went outside. The afternoon had been cold. Evening, which came early here because of the wall of rock to the west blocking the afternoon sunlight, made the air positively frigid. Alex turned up the collar of his buffalo coat and trudged down the block and onto the slope to reach the boardinghouse where he was to take his meals.

'You would be Mr Benton?' Alex asked the man who presided over the long dining hall.

'I am, sir.' Benton glanced at the empty sleeve and said, 'You must be Captain Adamley.'

'At your service, sir.'

Benton grunted. 'Your voice gives you away, Captain. You should know that this area was a hotbed of Unionists during the conflict.'

'Does that make a difference, Mr Benton?'

'To some it might. Though your disability might protect you.'

Alex bristled, the pad of muscle across his shoulders and at the back of his neck growing taut. 'I don't need that sort of protection, sir, and if it's trouble you're wanting — '

'Whoa. Don't be getting your back up with me, Captain. I'm a subject of her majesty the queen, and none of it made a lick nor a spittle of difference to me. I only wanted to warn you.'

'And so you have done, sir.' Alex tried, with limited success, to let his blood cool.

'There's a meal schedule posted over there, Captain,' Benton said, pointing. 'We start serving supper in twenty minutes. You can wait in the parlor there.' He pointed again.

'Fine. Thank you.' Even so, Alex was in a pugnacious humor when he entered the large parlor and chose a chair as far as he could get from the three other men already waiting there.

It was only after he'd sat and was staring at the flames' visible dancing beyond the cast-iron ventilation ring that he realized this was the first time he'd allowed himself an impulse that he would have considered perfectly natural and ordinary before that incident aboard the *Belle*. The first time he was ready to fight if need be. Or even to seek out a fight if that seemed the course he should lay.

Well, dammit, he was still a man. A man with but one arm perhaps, but a man nonetheless.

He hadn't had that sense lately. It pleased him to have it back now.

He reached for a ragged copy of the *Rocky Mountain News* that lay on a table nearby. It was an edition he'd already read when he was staying down at the O'Reillys' city house, but that was all right. He would read it again.

V

Alex was full as a tick in a dog's ear and indeed was content now in spite of his earlier surge of anger. Benton served a good meal. Alex had no idea how much the Rover paid for board in this house, but he had an idea they were getting good value for the money. This evening's supper had been no mere trotting out of the cheap and the filling. Instead of those time-honored boarding-house tricks, Gerald Benton put plenty of meat on the table. There had been a pot roast and stewed chicken alike and no limitation on how much of either, or both, the diners could take.

With his stomach warm and time on his hands — hand — for the weekend, Alex struggled into the heavy but very effective buffalo coat and fumbled with the buttons before heading down to the main street in search of something to top the evening off.

He found it in the nearest saloon.

The place was not fancy. Sawdust lay

thick on the floor to absorb whatever fluids might fall there, and three tables at the back of the long, narrow room were surrounded by men who were quietly intent on their card games. Off to the side near the back was a baize-covered table where a blond girl in a shockingly short dress was dealing monte for half a dozen loudly enthusiastic gamblers. Alex knew better than to put any faith in the honesty of monte play, but he couldn't help look twice at the dealer. Not only was her bottle-green dress hemmed above the knee, the low cut neck drooped open more than a little whenever she leaned forward to pitch her cards.

Alex smiled softly to himself. Smart girl. She knew damned good and well where the gents would have their attention while she manipulated the play. And it certainly was not on the cards. Only she paid close attention to those.

A free launch was laid out at the far end of the bar, and the trade was brisk enough to require the services of three bartenders to keep up with it all. The place smelled of pipe smoke and beer, and the room was filled with the din of dozens of conversations. There were probably fifty men there or more after the recent change of shift, most of them wearing the rough clothing, cloth caps, and sturdy shoes that Alex was already learning to associate with the miner's trade.

'Yes, sir, what can I get you?' a middle-aged bartender asked when Alex pressed his way close to the bar.

Alex grinned at him. Beer locally brewed down on the lowlands and bar whiskey made right here from alcohol and additives that a man was happiest not knowing was what he could expect in a place like this. He'd seen enough saloons in enough ports of call to know and be comfortable with that. 'Brandy, if you please,' he tossed out just to see how the barkeep would react.

The gent did not blink an eye. 'Calvados or Napoleon?' he asked.

'Calvados,' Alex spat out, taken quite aback by the choice.

The bartender had not been pulling Alex's leg, either. He brought a large bottle out from beneath the counter — it was a label Alex last saw in France — and poured a generous measure into a tin cup. Apparently practical considerations imposed certain limits to what was prudent here.

The man placed the cup onto the clean but unpolished bar top, and Alex reached into his pocket for one of the silver dollars he'd gotten earlier.

'No need for that, Captain Adamley. You're on a tab.'

'Thank you.' Was there no one in Holihan who did not yet know who the one-armed stranger was and what he was doing here?

Not that he was complaining. He lifted the cup close to his nose and inhaled the warm, fruity scent of the strong apple brandy, then took a very small sip of it. Nice. Very nice indeed, he judged.

He lifted the cup higher in a toast to

the barman, nodded, and smiled.

The brandy reached his stomach and spread its gentle warmth there.

Alex was as content as he could remember being in quite a long time.

VI

Alex chuckled softly to himself. He was standing beside the monte table, thoroughly enjoying the view into the dealer's decolletage, but discovered something rather interesting on the table also. Someone was actually winning. Someone, that is, other than the dealer, who up close was neither quite so young nor quite so pretty as she'd seemed from across the room.

Of the gamblers who drifted in and out of the play, there was one who slowly and unobtrusively but quite consistently won. He placed small bets only and dropped his winnings into a pocket instead of letting them pile up on the table before him. It was entirely possible, Alex thought, that even the dealer did not realize how often the old gentleman won, or she might have thwarted him, even if it cost her in the short term, just to get him to leave her table.

The fellow's method, Alex observed, was simple in the extreme. With so many bettors in play and only three cards to choose from, every card would be covered by bets for every deal. Someone therefore would win on every hand played while the majority would lose. The dealer would come out ahead, even if all else were equal.

Like any experienced dealer, though, this one wanted to take as much as possible and dealt accordingly.

One long, wet night in Portugal, Alex learned the secret of monte. Not that he could have dealt the game himself, not with two hands on his best day. But he'd had the method explained to him. And that was that the pay card — in this game the black queen standing in contrast to two red aces, although any combination of three contrasting cards was permissible — was held in the dealer's palm, only to be dropped when and how the dealer chose. Just like in the pea-and-shell game in which there was no pea under any shell until or unless the dealer placed it there long after the betting was done, there was more to be seen than the bettors ever knew. And for a good dealer, there was no gamble whatsoever. Wins and losses were merely a way for the dealer to move the play along, tossing out the enticing excitement of a win one time, raking in profit on the next.

This game of monte was no different. And in order to reap a steady income, the aging bettor who'd caught Alex's eye was waiting until the last moment before placing his coin, then tossing it onto the spot with the fewest other wagers. The dealer would almost invariably drop the queen onto the spot where she would have to pay out the least in winnings. The heavier piles would quickly slide into her pocket and out of sight.

Playing a dime at a time, never more than a quarter, the old man would make little profit. But it would indeed be a profit.

And before his slow but steady extraction from the play was noticed by the dealer, the old fellow nodded, tipped her a dime, and withdrew from the game.

Alex tossed back the last drops of the brandy he'd been carrying and turned to follow him.

'May I buy you a drink?' he offered when he caught up with the gent.

'Have we met?'

'No, sir.' Alex smiled. 'But I admire your play. I only thought to repay the pleasure you've given me from watching. If this is not a convenient time, sir, I shall withdraw.' He bowed slightly.

The old fellow laughed. 'Not at all. And thank you.' He led the way through the crowd to the front where a few tables and chairs were available.

VII

'Marc Anthony Jones,' the old fellow said when he introduced himself. 'And I thank you for the brandy, sir. To tell you the truth, I've been coming here for months and months but never knew they carried anything quite so fine.' He raised his glass in salute to his host and knocked back half the Calvados.

Alex took a much smaller sip and gave the old man his name.

'You noticed my play, you say?' Jones asked.

'Yes, sir.'

'Not many are so observant. I trust I can rely on you to keep mum about it?' He was smiling, but Alex could see he was at the same time quite serious in this request.

'Certainly.' Alex smiled also. 'But I may emulate you. With your permission, of course.'

'Feel free, young man. And the same trick works in other games as well, by the bye. Including the wheel of fortune.'

Alex looked around. 'I hadn't seen a wheel but — '

'Oh, not here. In the other establishments. I, um, play in them all, you see. Never take much in any of them at any one time. One must avoid the temptations of greed.'

'You supplement your income this way on a regular basis, I take it?' Alex asked.

'Young man, this *is* my income. I am too old to work underground, too unskilled for employment above-ground.'

'Nonsense, Mr Jones. You are an educated man and a gentleman of breeding. I can hear it in your voice. See it in your carriage.'

Jones began to guffaw. Loudly. 'Mr Adamley, for that I'll thank you twice over. But the truth is that I have no education save that I scraped out of books on my own and no breeding known, for I was an orphan and a foundling. I don't even know my true age, although I *think* I shall soon reach my full three score and ten. No, sir, I fear I've fooled you on both those counts.'

'I submit, Mr Jones, however you came by your education, you did obtain it. And while your ancestry may be unknown, without doubt yours is a noble lineage.'

'Gracious, Mr Adamley. I shall have to keep you close and induce you to repeat your opinions often, for every man enjoys a little flattery from time to time. One thing I would ask of you now, Mr Adamley.'

'Ask away. If I can satisfy your request, I shall certainly do so.'

'Oh, I believe you will be capable. My request, you see, is that you permit me this time to buy the next round.'

'Mr Jones, it would be ungracious of me to refuse your request. I accept.' He grinned. 'On condition that I be permitted the round to follow this one.'

'Done, sir, and done.' Jones rose and went to the bar to fetch the brandies.

Alex was in his cups — well, actually he was quite a distance past being merely in his cups — when finally he and Jones staggered out of the saloon, arm in arm and loudly singing sea chanties. The truth was that he was drunk as a lord. So much so that it was a wonder he found his way back to his new home instead of passing out in an alley and freezing to death overnight.

VIII

Alex's teeth ached and his hair hurt. He'd had hangovers in his time. This one was outstanding. His mouth tasted like he'd been gargling with bilgewater. How was it possible that something that tasted so wonderfully good last night was so vile on his tongue this morning? He needed something to drink. But not with alcohol in it this time, thank you. He'd puke before reaching the door if he tried to swallow any sort of liquor right now, and he was pretty sure he hadn't bought cleaning supplies yesterday.

He sat upright, the movement causing his head to throb and pound with each and every beat of his heart. His stomach rumbled, and he belched, the taste of the gases perfectly awful in his mouth. He had to do something, anything, to get rid of the nastiness there.

Yesterday he'd bought a small, hog-bristle brush to scrub his teeth with and a tin of patent tooth cleaning powder. But he had no idea where they were. His purchases had been delivered at some point during the evening, but everything lay now in a jumble of burlap sacks that were piled on the floor near the front door.

The promised stove had been delivered, too, along with several bushels of coal, but no fire had been laid, and the inside of the cabin was frigid. He needed . . . he needed a clear head, that was what he needed. Preferably a brand-new one, for he was fairly sure he'd ruined this one.

He stood, rather shakily, and stumbled

over to the bags that held his many purchases. He knew there was tea in there. Somewhere. But he had no water to make it with. Come to think of it, he hadn't remembered to buy a pail to carry water. Nor a keg to hold it once he fetched any. Dammit.

He gave up looking for the toothbrush and powder, squeezed a can of tomatoes between his knees and stabbed the top with his new kitchen knife. The juice the tomatoes were packed in tasted like nectar from on high, its acid cutting through the hair on his tongue and sluicing much of the foulness from his mouth.

'Better, better,' he mumbled to himself. But not so much better that he failed to yearn for one of the powders Dr Fredericks used to make up for him when he was in pain. He would cheerfully have swallowed a pint of those powders now if he had them. Which probably meant it was a very good thing that he had none lest he kill himself by ingesting too much.

Death, on the other hand, might well be a mercy.

Alex stood again, ignored the mess he was leaving behind, and staggered outside in search of the outhouse. Fortunately, he didn't have to worry about looking for his coat and struggling into it. He'd never taken it off when he passed out atop his bed last night.

IX

He ate lunch — he'd slept through breakfast and very nearly was late arriving for the midday set meal as well — and was amazed because he was able to keep it in his stomach. Food and a half gallon or so of steaming coffee did much to restore the inner man. So much so that he was able to walk upright when he left the boarding-house. Coming down to it, he'd been bent over and crab-like, fearful that a misstep would topple him and he would roll downhill and into a snowbank, not to be seen again until next spring. More or less.

Mm, yes. He was most definitely feeling better now that he was rested and fed.

After lunch, he went back down to the business district and corrected the errors of omission he'd made the day before, ordering a pail and keg, broom and mop to be put onto his account and taken up to his cabin to be piled on top of everything else already lying in disarray there. Soon, Alex realized, he would have to take a little time to paw through it all to see what he had and where to store it. In the cramped space aboard ship a man learns to be tidy with his personal possessions. That was a lesson Alex seemed quickly to have forgotten now that he was beached.

He belched — the flavor infinitely more bearable now than the morning's loathsome taste had been — and steeled himself to make another assault on the saloons of Holihan.

After all, he had started out yesterday with a mission in mind.

It was just that he'd been sidetracked by Marc Anthony Jones. All Jones's fault, of course. Um . . . of course.

Now, however, sober and serious once again, he would continue on the task he'd set for himself.

He would find the sons of bitches who'd assaulted him those weeks past.

X

Alex had no conscious memory of the men he'd briefly seen that day at Rattlesnake Hollow. He recalled only that there had been two of them and that they came out of one of the cabins as he walked by. He thought he might have spoken to them, but if either of them responded, he did not now remember it. Nor did he remember the first thing about what they looked like.

His hope was that he would recognize them when he saw them.

And in the meantime, he had the description Toby Madison gave him for the men Madison overheard in a saloon up here while Alex was still recovering down in the city. That description would make at least one of them easy enough to identify.

Blazing red hair, Toby said. One of the men at the table that night was tall and lean and had bright red hair. The other was shorter and nondescript, Madison said, with naught but a short beard with flecks of gray in it to make him stand out in a crowd. And of course a description as meager as that would make no one stand out in anything, particularly since a short beard can be gone and forgotten on a whim.

But the redhead . . . there were not so very many tall, skinny, redheaded men about.

Alex had tried to think back to the day he was beaten and robbed, and he could not make himself remember a red-haired man, no matter how hard he tried. The only explanation he could reach was that the fellow must have been wearing a hat or a cap, perhaps even one of those made of fur and with dangling ear flaps. Hats like that were fairly common here in the mountains, he was discovering, and they would certainly hide a man's hair color. Otherwise, he really would have thought he would remember at least that one of the pair.

When they robbed him, they left him for dead. Alex wondered if they knew by now that he'd survived the ordeal in spite of their best efforts. Certainly they would know if he encountered them here.

Alex wanted — damned well intended — to find them.

He had no idea what level of justice he could expect in this rough mining camp. He did know that he would not again allow himself to be their victim.

Rather, they should walk in fear of him, damn them.

He was done with moping about feeling sorry for himself. What he had lost, he'd come lately to realize, was an appendage. Nothing more. His heart and his nerve remained untouched by damn Yankee ball or surgeon's knife.

So let those men beware, and Henry Holihan, too, if he was the one behind the robbery.

6

I

Alex stepped out of one of the public outhouses situated beside the creek. Another man was waiting there.

'Sorry,' Alex apologized. It always took him a fairly long time because of the difficulty he had manipulating buttons one-handed.

The man did not move aside to allow Alex past. He looked, in fact, belligerent, presumably angry because he'd been waiting so long.

'If you would excuse me, please?' Alex said.

The scruffy, ragged, none too presentable man — he had hair so pale it looked almost white except for a three- or four-day growth of dark brown whiskers — shoved Alex in the chest. Hard. The impact of the unexpected push knocked Alex back onto his heels.

'Hey, now!'

The man pushed him again. Harder this time. And he followed the push by ducking low and planting his shoulder against Alex's chest, bulling forward so that Alex was carried backward, back inside the heavy, fetid stink of the outhouse.

'Stop, damn it,' Alex barked. His voice held the sharp edge of command in it, but this unkempt fellow ignored the order and, leaning forward with both hands firm on Alex's shoulders, tried to pin Alex to the wall.

'Give it over,' the fellow growled. His breath smelled of whiskey and vomit. 'Give it over, I'm tellin' you, or I'll dump you headfirst down this crapper.'

Alex did not think so. And he'd had just about enough of being set upon by robbers.

Abruptly, he dropped onto the wooden bench built over the cess pit in the outhouse, moving underneath his assailant's grip instead of doing the expected thing and trying to push against it. The man's hands remained on Alex's shoulders, but he no longer had the leverage to keep Alex immobilized.

'Hey!' the would-be robber yelped.

He howled again, and much louder, when Alex's balled fist plunged wrist deep into the target placed so conveniently before him, that being the robber's unprotected crotch.

The man's face became suddenly as pale as his hair, and his expression took on that slack disinterest of numbing agony.

Alex placed his hand flat on the fellow's breastbone and pushed, fending him off and sending him reeling backward, out of the outhouse and onto the rock-strewn footing behind the saloons and downtown businesses.

Before the man could recover his senses, Alex regained his feet and rushed after him. He buried another punch in the soft pit of the fellow's stomach and kneed him hard in the face when he doubled over in response.

Alex heard the rather satisfying crunch of breaking cartilage, and the robber's shattered nose and upper lip began spraying blood.

Alex raised his foot, intent on putting the boots to this man, fully intending to stomp his head, his neck, his kidneys . . . whatever he could reach.

He stopped only because someone grabbed him from behind.

Alex spun around and threw a hard, sweeping punch in response to this new assault.

II

'Leave be, damnit. You've beat him; you don't have to kill him, too. Now. Can I let go of you? Are you all right? Ready to calm down?'

'I . . . yeah. Sorry, Toby. I didn't know it was you.'

Madison grinned and dabbed a fingertip at the corner of his mouth. It came away red where Alex had split it.

'It isn't bleeding bad,' Alex said.

Madison grunted. He did not seem to resent the punch though. 'I'll say one thing for you, Adamley. You can still fight.'

Alex wasn't so sure about that. He was trembling in the aftermath of an outburst of furious energy. He felt weak in the knees, and his breath was ragged and quick.

Madison looked at the man who was still writhing on the ground behind Alex. 'What should we do with him?'

'Are there any police here? A town marshal, maybe?'

Toby shook his head. 'No. We have mine security, that's all. Each outfit handles its own.'

'I want to question this man, Toby. He was trying to rob me. Could be for the same reason I was beaten and robbed before.'

Madison raised an eyebrow. 'You mean there was a reason other than just taking what you had in your pockets?'

'I don't know that, Toby. Not for sure. But I think . . . Yes, I think there might have been. That's why I want to talk with this piece of shit. I really don't care about charging him with anything, like in a court or anything, but I damn sure want to get some answers from him.'

'We can arrange that easy enough. Why don't you wait here, Alex. Make sure this ol' boy doesn't go anyplace. I'll go find some of our security people. Whatever is going on here, we'll get to the bottom of it.'

'Fine. Thank you.'

Toby hurried through an alley to reach the street. Alex leaned over, gasping for air, while on the ground in front of him the robber lay groaning softly.

It was about time that he would get some answers, he thought.

And he did intend to get those answers, whether this man wanted to give them or not.

III

Alex was shaken when he walked out of the Irish Rover's security office. He'd thought he knew something about brutality. He'd sailed a good many seas and known a good many ports. He had seen what the gendarmes in Marsailles could do to a man who annoyed them, and once he had personally experienced the ferocity of the copper-button bobbies who prowled the wharves of Liverpool.

But he had never seen cold viciousness like that displayed by Dan Tyler, who was the Rover's chief of security.

By the time Tyler was satisfied he knew everything the robber could possibly tell him, Alex was half sick just from watching the man work. Quite early in the interrogation he found himself feeling sorry for the robber. In comparison, his own attempt to batter the man's cods to mush seemed almost a friendly gesture.

But the fellow did open right up and

spill everything he knew.

No, sir, he didn't know who the gentleman there was and hadn't seen him before, sir, and hadn't targeted him special, sir, but just waited for whoever stepped out of that shitter, sir, and tried to rob him so's he could have money to buy something to eat . . . Ah, sir, don't do that again, please, sir, I'm begging you . . . So's he could buy liquor, that was the truth of it, because he did like his bottle awful well, sir, and it'd got him fired from the Big H just a couple days back, see, and he was thinking about going on up to Bailey or Fairplay, for they said a man could find work there, sir, but he wasn't ready to go just yet for he wanted to have a little more fun here first but they'd cut off his credit when they found out he'd been fired and . . . No, sir, I'm sorry, sir, please, please, *please!*

The robber's name was Jared Thomas. He was thirty-six years old and came from Indiana, and he hadn't taken any part in that earlier robbery and knew nothing about it. No one hired him. No one told him to rob Captain Adamley nor to try to take any particular item from him. All he wanted was money.

It would not have bothered him if his victim died as a result of the robbery. In fact, it would have been a good thing if he did, because then there would be no one to identify him as the robber.

Even hearing that little detail hadn't been enough to harden Alex's heart to the point of wanting to see any more of Dan Tyler's methods, no matter how effective they proved to be.

But he did have the information. Now he knew. 'Toby.'

'Yes?'

'Tell them to turn the poor son of a bitch loose, will you please?'

'Of course. We don't have any authority to hold him.'

'Tell them to do it while he's still alive, please.'

'He will be. I can promise you that.'

'Thank you, Toby.'

'Are you all right? You don't look so

good. Do you want to see a doctor?'

'No, I'm just . . . a little queasy, that's all.'

'If you change your mind, just let me know. We have a fellow who works for the Rover. He isn't a regular doctor. Truth is, he's a barber-surgeon. But he's pretty good. Real good with sewing up cuts and stopping bleeding and that sort of thing.' Madison smiled. 'And he gives a good shave or haircut, too.'

'I'll keep that in mind, Toby. Thanks.'

'Is there anything else I can do for you?'

'No. I . . . appreciate your help.' He wished now that he hadn't asked for it, that Tyler hadn't done the things that he did, but that wasn't Madison's fault, and in any case, it was too late to go back now and change anything.

And if it were possible to step back in time and change things, it wouldn't be anything concerning some out-of-work small-time robber that Alex would choose to change.

'By the way,' Madison said, 'I almost

forgot the reason I came looking for you this afternoon.'

'Yes?'

'You're invited to Sunday dinner with the O'Reillys. Miss Beth said you're to come about two. Dinner won't be served until six or thereabouts, so my advice would be to make sure you eat lunch before you show up, or you'll get awful hungry waiting for the meal t' be served.'

'I'll be there.' He was glad now that he'd purchased that suit and tie. 'Thanks.'

Madison touched the bill of his cap. 'Watch your back, Captain.'

Yes, Alex thought, he would have to do that. He turned and began walking downhill toward town, while Madison headed for the mine headquarters.

IV

The tussle with Jared Thomas from Indiana had taught Alex something.

Several somethings in fact.

One of those was that he was still capable of fighting back if accosted.

The other thing was that he was no longer nearly as capable as he'd been when he had two hands with which to punch and grapple.

Trying to engage in a fistfight one-handed was possible. It was not efficient.

And if there had been two men opposing him, the blunt truth was that he would not have had a chance.

Two men who, unlike Mr Thomas, knew what they were doing in the rough and tumble? Even less of a hope.

No, if there were any chance at all that he might have to brace two men in order to find out who hired them to rob him — as Alex firmly believed had been done — he needed more than his still very awkward left hand to oppose them.

From the security office he went immediately down to the business district and sought out the friendly proprietor who'd already been so helpful.

'No, sir, I'm afraid not,' the gentleman said in response to Alex's inquiry, 'but I think Carson Greve carries those. His store is in the next block. You can't miss it. He has an anvil suspended over the sidewalk in front of his store.'

'Oh, I remember that all right. Always walk wide of it just in case it might fall,' Alex said.

The storekeeper laughed. 'Nearly everybody does that. Want to know a secret? The anvil is a fake. It's really made out of wood covered over with a thin coat of lead and painted black.'

'I'll be damned.' Alex thanked the man and went down the street to Greve's hardware to repeat his request.

'Sure, I can help you.' He looked at the empty sleeve, then shifted his gaze back to Alex's face. 'Mind if I make a suggestion?'

'Please do.'

'It'd be hard as hell to load a regular revolver with just the one hand. You got to tip the powder in and set the ball in place and then ram it in snug, rotate the cylinder, and set the caps in place. It isn't easy, even with two hands.'

'I'm afraid I know that already,' Alex said, 'but even so, a revolving cylinder pistol beats hell out of any other pocket gun.'

'Not all of them,' Greve told him. 'I happen to have two of the Smith and Wesson revolvers that use self-contained cartridges.'

'I never heard of them.'

'Let me show you.'

The little pistols were not impressive to look at. They were of small caliber and unimposing size. But they did indeed fire self-contained ammunition that had a brass outer casing, powder inside where it would be fully protected from dampness, and lead bullets seated at the open end. The back end enclosed some sort of priming charge that would explode when struck and induce the cartridge to fire.

'No, sir. I never saw such a thing. But I think I like it.'

'To reload, you slip this catch and tip

the barrel downward. That exposes the cylinder. Just dump out the spent cases and drop in new ones.'

Alex grunted. If he had to reload this gun in a hurry, he could clamp it beneath what was left of his right arm — he was becoming good at holding things there — and push the fresh cartridges in with his hand.

'I definitely like it. I'll take it, thank you. And some of those cartridges, too, of course. How many did you say come in a box?'

'Fifty.'

'Give me three boxes, please.'

Greve raised his eyebrow, and Alex laughed. 'I don't intend any mayhem. Just want to be able to practice so I'm familiar with the gun.'

'My only advice to you, friend, is that you be careful who you shoot. With a bullet this small, it wouldn't do to hit anybody. You might make him mad.'

Alex laughed again. But there was more than a germ of truth in the caution. The little weapon would have no stopping power.

With luck, of course, he would never need to use it. But he very much liked the idea of having it in his pocket.

Just in case.

V

Alex slept late on Sunday morning. But then he'd been up late as well, wandering from saloon to saloon in a fruitless search for the red-haired man and his companion. He still believed he would recognize them when he saw them, conscious memory or no.

But he hadn't yet seen them, dammit.

Once again, he was too late for breakfast, but Sunday dinner at the boardinghouse was so good, he didn't mind that in the slightest.

Madison had said he should stoke up with a good noontime feed, so he dug deep into the chicken and dumplings, the pot roast, the mashed potatoes and gravy, and the soft rolls still warm from the oven, all of it tender enough that he did not have to worry about the embarrassment of trying to cut his meat. Even the beef pot roast was falling-apart tender and could be enjoyed without benefit of a knife.

The table was full, one diner sitting down to eat as soon as another got up to leave. Alex gathered that there was no shift working on Sunday, which effectively doubled the number of men who would be above ground for the Sunday meals. During the week, a good half of the boarders would be engaged in their twelve-hour shifts at any given time.

Alex knew no one at the boarding-house and remained silent, save for occasionally asking that a dish be passed.

A stilled tongue, however, did not block his ears. He was about to reach for a tempting apple pan dowdy when he overheard a snatch of conversation that took away any appetite he had left.

' . . . heard he'd been beat near to death even before he was dumped into the creek . . . '

' . . . alive when they done it, too.'

'Froze damn near solid, is what I heard.'

'Poor son of a bitch. I expect nobody knows who he was.'

'I do. Johnny Margett told me this morning he seen the body with his own eyes. Said it was Jerry Thomas that Johnny and me used to work with over at the Big H before we came here.'

'That so?'

'That's what Johnny said, an' he knew Jerry as good as I ever did. Said it wasn't no accident, him being in the water an' freezing like that. Said he was beat something awful first.'

'That's what I heard too. They say . . . '

Alex didn't listen to the rest of that conversation. He dropped his fork and spoon onto his plate and stumbled away from the table. Behind him, someone barked that he should clear his plate like anybody else, but Alex paid the complaint no mind. He felt sick to his stomach.

Jared Thomas had been released alive all right, just like Toby Madison and that SOB security chief Dan Tyler promised.

But it had been done in such a way that the failed robber was sure to freeze to death overnight.

It was not a thing Alex could take any pleasure in, regardless of Thomas's callous unconcern for Alex's own fate.

Damn it anyway.

He pulled his coat on and hurried outside into the clean, quiet air.

VI

He was late for Sunday dinner with the O'Reillys. He'd started the process of dressing in perfectly good order. Or so he'd thought at the time. It was the damned necktie that almost defeated him.

Even with the patent hook-and-eye closure, it proved almost impossible for him to tuck the fabric under his collar. He'd eventually ended up unbuttoning his shirt and taking it and the celluloid collar off again so he could stuff the tie in place before putting the shirt on. Then he pulled the two ends of the bow tie together and manipulated the tiny hook into the impossibly small metal eye.

With two hands it would have been the sort of simple task that is performed a hundred times a day without requiring conscious thought.

With but one hand, it was a mountain of frustration that had to be overcome with dexterity and — more important — with persistence.

As it was, he was twenty minutes or so late arriving at the big white house that was as close as Holihan came to having a mansion.

'Captain Adamley! How nice of you to come.' It was Beth O'Reilly herself who met him at the door. That

230

surprised him. Pleased him, too. It was in a way a very nice compliment. 'Come in, please.'

She led him to the parlor where her brother was already enjoying whiskey and a pipe in the company of Toby Madison, a gentleman named Conrad — first name or last, Alex never did quite get clear — and a priest named Father Flaherty. Conrad turned out to be a mining engineer who may well have been a genius as an engineer but who was clearly uncomfortable with the social niceties. So much so that he came across as taciturn to the point of sullenness. Alex suspected the truth was that Conrad was merely shy. Very.

Father Flaherty was quite the opposite, voluble and loud and seeking to dominate the conversation, most of which seemed to revolve around the beauty and the glories of auld Ireland. Alex thought the priest to be drunk. Perhaps chronically so.

The good thing was that neither he

nor Conrad was required to contribute much to the gathering. Nodding and smiling seemed quite enough to fulfill their end of things.

Beth O'Reilly was demure and for the most part silent. She was also quite beautiful. Relieved of the burden of participating in the conversation, Alex spent most of the time peering at Beth.

It was not at all an unpleasant way to pass the time.

After several hours of listening to Flaherty pontificate, Beth relieved the monotony by playing a few piano selections. The girl played remarkably badly. But goodness gracious, she did look good when poised, back straight and chin high, on the bench.

Alex liked it all the more that from where he sat in a softly cushioned leather chair, he could see the slim, tidy shape of her ankles when she worked the pedals.

Eventually, they were summoned to dinner by a plump, freckle-faced, red-haired Irish maid.

The meal was fine, but in truth no better than what Alex enjoyed earlier at the boardinghouse. The food was plain. Lamb. Potatoes. Carrots. Onions. It was filling but not elegant, even in presentation.

Afterward, when the gentlemen were repairing to the library for whiskey and cigars, Beth drew Alex aside.

'Captain, I don't want to offend you, but . . . could I mention a subject of some delicacy?'

'Of course.'

'I noticed . . . forgive me, but during dinner I noticed . . . well . . . your fingernails.'

'Yes?'

'They are uneven and . . . forgive me, please . . . not clean.'

Alex felt a flush of heat in his cheeks. He had a rather good excuse for the condition of his nails. The only method of caring for them open to him was gnawing at them with his teeth, something he'd never done before in his life. But the simple truth was that she was quite correct. They were indeed ragged and filthy.

'Would it offend you, Captain, if I were to trim and clean them for you?' Her eyelashes looked half a foot long when she shyly lowered them.

'I couldn't ask — '

'But you have not asked, sir. It is I who have offered.' And so, while the other gentlemen drank and smoked, Alex reveled in intimate closeness to this lovely young woman who gently and patiently took his hand in hers and attended to him with nippers and files and cuticle scissors.

He wished the evening would continue like that forever. Or at least until he felt it safe to stand upright without his male reaction to such beauty becoming embarrassingly obvious.

On the whole, questions of food and entertainment aside, Alex considered Sunday dinner with the O'Reillys to be a roaring success.

VII

Alex had difficulty sleeping that night. He was tired enough. No question about that. But his thoughts kept leaping along rather wildly unseemly lines back to Beth O'Reilly. To the look of her. The scent of her. The feel of her hand soft and gentle upon his.

To have her perform so intimate a task . . . this was no simple charity she offered. It was tantamount to a declaration of very personal interest in him.

Wasn't it?

Ah, that was the question that alternately inflamed and shattered him.

Did she truly mean to announce such interest? Whenever Alex found himself believing that, he was aroused almost to bursting. He'd been crippled by those damn Yankee balls; he had not been unmanned. And the thought of Beth O'Reilly . . .

He would think that, but moments later he would become equally convinced that he misinterpreted the beautiful young woman's intentions. She was only offering a kindness to a cripple. She could not possibly take amorous interest in a man with so little prospect . . . and so little physical ability . . . as he. He was deluding himself. He was a fool. He was being unrealistic. He was pathetic. He was . . .

His thoughts would reverse themselves in an instant and once more he would believe — ardently, passionately, desperately believe — that Beth indeed did intend to send exactly that message. She was interested. Even attracted. She was . . .

She was as far beyond his reach as the moon and the stars. She was beautiful. She was elegant. She was gloriously desirable.

And Alex Adamley, late of the Confederate States of America naval merchant service, was a damned fool.

She had feelings for him. She did not.

Alex got scant sleep indeed that long night through.

VIII

It was, he quickly discovered, not necessarily a gold mine if you owned a gold mine.

That is, the reality of owning a gold mine was not at all the same thing as the popular perception of it, certainly was not the same as the common expression, 'It's a gold mine,' to designate something as being lucrative and desirable.

The Irish Rover, Alex very quickly discovered, was not a high-paying proposition.

Once he began poring over the company ledgers, he found that the Rover barely broke even. And in some months it went into the red.

'Where would I find the early records?' he asked his new assistant, a small, clerkish man named John Barkley. Barkley had welcomed him with very poorly disguised hostility this Monday morning and was spending at least half his time glaring at Alex from his cramped desk over at the side of the room.

Barkley hesitated for several long moments before he responded, and then he gave no more assistance than to jerk his chin in the direction of a chest-high steel vault that stood open at the back of the office.

'Thank you, John.' Alex gave the man a huge, deliberately cheerful smile. If the man wanted to be a sourpuss, that was fine, but he would have to do it while being overwhelmed with a show of friendliness from Alex.

Probably, Alex thought, Barkley believed that he should have been made office manager instead of this newcomer. The man no doubt viewed Alex as an interloper and an intruder.

Alex had no problem with that. He'd had to deal with disgruntled ship's officers often enough in the past, more than a few of them downright incompetent as well. Certainly John Barkley seemed both knowledgeable and competent when it came to the Rover's accounting needs. Alex suspected he would not be nearly as difficult to deal with as Barkley himself seemed to want.

And it was very likely also, he concluded, that this sour disposition was the reason why Barkley was passed over in favor of Alex.

That and . . . dare he consider it as a real possibility? . . . that and Beth O'Reilly's personal interest in having Alex nearby.

He set that thought aside to be pondered and worried over later and went to find the original cash flow ledgers for the Irish Rover. He wanted to familiarize himself with the business operation from the outset. And in the meantime, John Barkley was more than capable of tending to the operation's immediate needs.

IX

'Care to join me for dinner?' He smiled. Broadly. Unrelentingly cheerful. And he would continue that way if it damn well killed him. 'My treat, John.'

The response was predictable. The same he'd received when he invited Barkley to lunch earlier. The man grunted something inaudible — probably just as well that it was, he supposed — and sat with his nose in a ledger, not even looking up as Alex tidied the big desk that was now his.

Alex finished clearing off the desk and carefully locked the top drawer. There was nothing in it that was private or personal, but he was curious about something. He plucked a bit of lint from the dangling right sleeve of his shirt and draped it over a corner of the drawer. If Barkley opened the drawer to get a look at what Alex had been doing today, Alex would know about it tomorrow.

'Sure you won't come along?' Alex invited as he pulled his coat on and struggled with the buttons. 'Last chance.'

Barkley did not even bother to grunt this time but ignored Alex utterly.

'Good night, John. See you in the morning.'

In a way, Alex was disappointed that the assistant chose not to come. He really would have liked to have someone with whom he could discuss the development of the Irish Rover's business as he'd come to see it after a day inspecting the books.

Granted that he knew virtually nothing about mining, prudence and common sense are the same whether a man's business is the extraction of minerals from the ground or the transport of goods across a sea. You have a service to offer, a payroll to meet, expenses charged against income. Ultimately you have to make sure that your income exceeds your outgo. It is a simple enough equation, regardless of the nature of the venture.

You have to bring in more than you put out, or you will not succeed.

And Kenneth O'Reilly's Irish Rover mine was no longer succeeding.

It was wildly successful in its earliest

days. Gold practically poured out of the ground and into O'Reilly's pockets.

But that was then.

More recently, the gold production was dramatically less than it had been. Just as many men were required in order to dig the ore, but the ore quality now was considerably poorer. The ore once yielded twenty-five, thirty, on some days as much as thirty-six ounces of processed gold to the ton of raw ore extracted. Those were the halcyon days for the Rover and the O'Reillys. More recently, though, the yield was consistently below ten ounces. More and more it paid out at eight, seven, even six ounces.

That really would not have been a problem, Alex thought, except the Irish Rover continued at or near the old levels of spending.

Even though income was drastically reduced, Kenneth O'Reilly continued to pay himself a more than generous salary. And his sister Beth had an open account upon which she drew freely and often. She was as extravagant as she was pretty.

The house in Denver and all its expenses were charged against the Rover's business accounts. The company paid out large sums as wages for security personnel and unspecified 'special security expenditures' that were charged and paid but not otherwise explained.

Alex wanted to know more before he approached Ken O'Reilly with any recommendations. He wanted to be sure of his facts. But his initial inclination would be to tell the man that he needed to make deep spending cuts. Security came immediately to mind as a possible savings target. But so, too, did Beth's free spending practices, and Alex was not at all sure how well that advice would be received.

It was none of his business what Beth O'Reilly chose to spend. But if Alex were going to serve as an effective and helpful manager, he felt obligated to give his employer honesty, even if it were unwelcome.

Without some changes in the spending practices, Alex was already convinced, the Irish Rover would bankrupt itself and cease to exist as a viable business entity. It would have to shut down. And then where would the O'Reillys be?

He hoped Kenneth was a sensible enough businessman to see the necessity when Alex pointed it out to him.

But that would not be tonight.

Alex paused at the door to glance back at Barkley, who continued to pretend that the new office manager was not there.

Then he walked out into the chill mountain twilight and down toward Holihan's business district. He wanted to get an early start this evening on his search for the redheaded man who might — or might not — know something about the robbery and beating Alex suffered.

X

He could find no redheaded man. Dammit! He went from saloon to saloon, not even taking time out to go to the boardinghouse for dinner. Instead, he settled for the dry cheese and hard, fly-blown slices of ham that were offered on one free lunch after another.

He sipped at a succession of beers, never bothering to finish any of them. The purchases were only an excuse for him to stand at the bar, nibble at pickled eggs and pig's feet, and look for a redheaded man to walk in.

It did not happen.

About nine-thirty, his stomach gurgling in protest of such treatment, Alex greeted Marc Anthony Jones. This was the third saloon in which he'd encountered Jones, but he hadn't wanted to intrude on the old man's livelihood while he was busy at the gaming tables. Now Jones appeared to be done fleecing the fleecers, at least for this particular evening.

'Can I buy you a beer, Mr Jones?'

'No thank you, Mr Adamley.' Jones smiled. 'I've noticed that you move from place to place almost as much as I do, although not for the same reason. Whatever your reason, Mr Adamley, it has nothing to do with strong drink. You rarely finish anything.'

'You're observant,' Alex said.

Jones shrugged. 'If curiosity is a curse, then I've been so abused. Now tell me, sir. Would your offer of a beverage extend to tea? I know a café where they brew a fine cup.'

'I . . . ' Alex paused. 'I was going to say that I would die for a cup of good tea. But that would be a lie. It would be pointless, wouldn't it? I might, however, consider killing for a cup.'

Jones laughed. 'No need for that. Come with me.'

He led the way outside and three blocks down, almost to the end of the Holihan business district before he turned right onto a footbridge that crossed the stream that had carved the canyon into the mountains here. It was the first time Alex had been on the Big H side of the canyon, and he felt vaguely uncomfortable about it, considering that it was Henry Holihan's Big H that Alex threatened with his deed. The redheaded man, after all, was one of Holihan's employees.

Still, this might be the opportunity he needed to find the man.

Jones took him to a cabin set close beside the bank of the creek. There was no sign outside to suggest that the place was anything more than a dwelling, but when they got inside, he found tables and chairs and a plump and cheerful blond woman in charge. There were no other customers at the moment.

'You're early, Marcus,' she greeted.

'I've had a good night of it, Maggie. Made all the more so because my young friend here insists on paying for my tea. And a drop of it for himself as well, if you please.'

'Tea it shall be, Marcus. And your usual?'

'Please.'

The usual turned out to be scones and blackberry jam. Maggie brought a plate heavy with the scones, which Alex dearly loved.

'Maggie makes the jams herself,' Marc said with a proprietary smile at the woman. 'So don't be thinking she's merely a pretty face. The girl can cook, too.'

Maggie blushed and slapped at him with the hem of her apron, but it was easy enough to see that the compliment pleased her. 'Go on with you, y' old fool.'

'Foolish I may be. Old I most certainly am. But a judge of scones . . . Mr Adamley tell me, do you or do you not agree?'

'Best scones I've had in years,' Alex affirmed. 'The finest jam as well, if I may say so.'

Maggie giggled and scurried away into her kitchen, which was separated from the dining area by a blanket nailed over the doorway.

Alex enjoyed another scone and helped himself to a second cup of tea. Marc was right, the tea was perfectly steeped and was served with a thick cozy over the pot to hold the heat. He thought for a moment before saying, 'Mr Jones, you are an observant man.'

'I try to be,' Marc agreed.

'You might help me.'

'Certainly. If I can.'

Alex did not want to get into long explanations. He said only, 'I would like to find a redheaded gentleman in town here. I'm told he works for the Big H mine in their security department.'

'Red-haired, you say?' Jones shook his head. 'Alex, my young friend . . . May I call you Alex? Thank you. Alex, I think I have seen every single resident of Holihan, whoever he might work for and whatever he may do. I do not personally know everyone. But I believe I am at least familiar with each. And as it happens, I know the Big H guards. They're a pleasant lot, and my bladder keeps me up at strange hours. Sometimes I drop in at the guard shack in the middle of the night, just to visit and play a little chess with their chief, Bill Edwards.

'And I can tell you with certainty, Alex, that there is no red-haired man who works in security at the Big H. Not one.'

Alex frowned. Toby Madison clearly described the two men he'd overheard. He also said he recognized them both as being Holihan's men.

'There are several red-haired men in Holihan, Alex, but none of them works in security. I am quite sure of that.'

Marc had no reason to lie about this. Nor any idea why Alex brought up the subject.

But the old gentleman certainly had the ability to confuse. And he most assuredly had just now done so.

'Thank you,' Alex said as he absently reached for another scone without noticing they'd already emptied the plate. 'Thank you very much.'

XI

Alex greeted John Barkley with an effusive good cheer that failed to put a dent in the man's sour nature, then unbuttoned his coat and hung it on a rack near the office door. He did not approach his desk but headed instead for the steep staircase leading to Kenneth O'Reilly's aerie. He tapped politely on the closed door and waited for an invitation to enter before he did so.

'Yes, Adamley?' Kenneth was seated behind a magnificent polished oak desk that must have taken block and tackle to lift into this office. Toby Madison was there with him, sitting in a much less impressive straight chair. Both men had coffee, and there was a plate on a corner of the desk with fried crullers white with sprinkles of refined sugar.

'I'm glad to find you both here,' Alex said. 'I need to speak with each of you, although on different topics.'

'Then join us, please. Care for some

coffee? A snack perhaps?' O'Reilly pointed to the crullers.

'No thank you.' He'd just had breakfast. Besides, he had something of a nervous stomach, anyway, from worrying about what he needed to tell Ken O'Reilly . . . and to ask Toby Madison. He sat stiffly in a chair that matched Madison's.

'What's on your mind?' O'Reilly invited.

Alex took a deep breath. Then told him. Not in great detail but certainly enough to give the man a fair warning that his business was in trouble.

'And you believe you can determine all that after a single day on the job, Adamley?'

'Yes, of course. I don't have detailed recommendations to offer at this point, Mr O'Reilly, but I had time enough to make a preliminary judgment yesterday. I think you have a problem, sir. Believe me, there are things I would much prefer to discuss with you. It is in fairness to you and your sister that I decided to speak up now. Naturally, you know this business far better than I. That is why I'm hoping that you can find means and methods to resolve the problems. You can probably do this much more quickly than I can. At this point, sir, I only want to warn you. Naturally, I stand ready to pursue the situation more closely so I can offer specific remedies in the very near future.'

O'Reilly steepled his fingertips and peered into the shadows between his two palms for a moment. Then he grunted. 'Very good, Adamley. Thank you. I'll look into this immediately. I, uh, believe you said you need to speak with Toby also?'

'Yes, sir, although this isn't in the line of business. It is something personal. Do you mind if I bring it up on company time?'

'Go right ahead, Adamley. Would you like to have your discussion in private? I can leave, if you wish.'

'No sir, but thank you. I wouldn't ask

you to leave your own office.' He turned to Madison. 'It's about the man you said you overheard talking about . . . well, possibly about the assault on me. You said he is a tall, red-headed man who works for the Big H's security. Are you sure about this? Because, you see, I've been told there is no such man employed in security there.'

XII

Alex went home to his cabin after supper at the boardinghouse that evening. Considering what Marc Anthony Jones told him, there was no need for him to continue searching Holihan for the tall, redheaded man.

And considering what Toby Madison told him, there was some pondering that he needed to do.

Madison had been offhand and dismissive of Jones's information. Whoever Alex spoke with was mistaken, that was all. Or to give that person the benefit of the doubt, it could be that the redheaded man Madison heard and recognized no longer worked for the Big H, although he certainly used to. Madison claimed he did not know the fellow's name, but he thought it was Joe something-or-other. Joe, Joseph, something like that.

The words had a hollow sound to them. Now. A week ago, Alex would have accepted them at face value and considered them gospel. Now he was not so sure.

He knew what a sharp and observant man Marc Anthony Jones was. Alex doubted Jones would give him false information, and if he did not know something, he would surely say that he did not. Marc had no reason to lie.

For that matter, Toby Madison had no reason to lie, either.

Did he?

Alex stirred the ashes of last night's fire until he found some live coals, opened the flue, then dragged the scuttle near and carefully fed fresh coal atop the old. He built a roaring fire before he turned the flue to nearly closed and then banked his fire so it would continue to warm the cabin through the night.

That done, he trimmed his beard and mustache and washed before going to bed.

Not that he expected to get much sleep, despite the early hour.

He had quite a lot of thinking to do.

XIII

'Miss Beth wants to see you. Down at the house.' Barkley sounded pleased when he delivered the message. Bad news, Alex guessed. Or at least Barkley was hoping it would be.

Alex took his coat back off the rack where he'd just hung it and struggled into it again. The morning was bitterly cold. He'd taken the trouble to feed and bank the fire in his cabin stove this morning in the hope the place would not be quite so frigid when he returned after work.

A storm seemed to be approaching in the low, dark clouds overhead. Already a light snow was drifting down when he took the path that led to town and to the O'Reillys' big house. Toby Madison opened the door to his knock, and Alex stamped his feet on the rug outside to make sure he did not track any of the snow indoors. Madison brought Alex into the parlor and remained, sitting off to one side.

Beth was radiantly lovely this morning. To look at her in her filmy gown with its low-cut neckline and a delicate cameo tied tight at her throat on a ribbon, one would not suspect that outdoors the weather was becoming so vile. Alex could hear a keening wind battering at the windows, but indoors there was only a cozy warmth radiating from the stoves that softly purred in practically every room.

Charles came in, refreshed the coal in

the parlor stove, and silently withdrew.

Beth waited until Charles was gone, then nodded to Toby, who quickly stood and followed Charles in the direction of the kitchen.

'Thank you for coming, Captain.' Her voice was low and intimately throaty, making her otherwise very ordinary comment sound as if he'd had a choice, as if he were a friend — or a suitor? — and not an employee.

After the many worrisome thoughts he'd had through the past night, Alex was not quite so pleased with her tone as he might have been.

If Toby Madison deliberately misled him about that overheard conversation, what possible reason could he have . . . unless Beth or Kenneth O'Reilly had a hand in it or at the very minimum knew of the deception? Alex did not for a moment question Madison's loyalty to the O'Reillys and the Irish Rover. And his statements were in stark contrast with the observations made by Marc Jones.

Now this. Alex found himself this morning more wary of Beth than smitten with her.

He was probably being foolish. But even so . . . 'Kenny told me about your conversation yesterday, Captain,' Beth said now.

'Yes?'

She smiled, the expression bright and vivid but, he thought, lacking something. Sincerity perhaps? 'I knew you were intelligent, Captain. Very much so. That is what I told Kenny to begin with. And I was right. It took you practically no time at all to see what we need to do in order to recover from the problems we've drifted into.'

A blind illiterate could have determined the same things just as quickly, Alex believed. But he did not say so.

'I am more grateful to you than you can imagine, Captain,' the lovely girl babbled on. 'I want . . . please forgive me for being so forward . . . but I am terribly attracted to intelligence and purpose in a man. Do I startle you,

Captain?' Her smile flashed brightly again. Bright as a star in a night sky far at sea. But as cold. That was it, he realized. Her smile was dazzling as any star he'd ever seen but gave off no warmth. All the warmth in this room came from that stove in the corner. 'Am I being too bold? Please forgive me.'

She lowered her chin and allowed her eyelashes to flutter, quick and delicate as a butterfly's wings.

Instead of being entranced — which he suspected was the girl's intention — Alex found himself wondering if Beth practiced this posture or if it came naturally to her.

She was a coquette, he saw now, and no more true than a portrait painted onto canvas.

She wanted something from him. Something that was very important to her.

Yesterday, the day before yesterday, Alex undoubtedly would have leaped to give this girl anything that would again bring a smile to that lovely face.

Today . . . it would depend.

She was looking at him intently, he saw. Judging the effect she was having on him? Probably. She leaned back in her chair. She smiled again, less brightly this time but more genuinely. She sat for a few moments as if in thought.

'You are indeed a very capable man, Captain Adamley. You impress me.'

'Thank you.' What else could he possibly say? But that was all he chose to say at the moment.

'I would like you to do a great service for me, Captain, and for my brother.'

'If I can, certainly.' He meant that. Up to a point.

'We intend to adopt your suggestions,' she said. 'Your reforms, if one could call them that. They are sensible, and Kenny and I believe they will bring us back to profitability. In the meantime, we need operating capital.'

Beth tugged a bell cord beside her chair, and a few moments later, both Toby and Charles entered the room. 'Please sit down, Toby. I want you to hear this. Charles, I would like tea.'

'Yes'm.' Charles bobbed his head and went back to the kitchen. Toby returned to the chair he'd occupied earlier.

'As I was just explaining to Captain Adamley, Toby, the Irish Rover is in need of operating capital. The captain has developed a reorganization plan that we intend to implement immediately.'

What Alex had mentioned to Kenneth was more along the lines of simple observation and commonsense suggestion. Certainly those thoughts were not yet assembled into anything so complete as a reorganization. At least he did not think them complete. But then it was clear to him by now that neither Kenneth nor Beth was particularly well versed in the needs of business. As for their common sense, he was in no position to judge, never mind any suspicions that were beginning to form.

'I want you to drive Captain Adamley to Denver, Toby. I need Charles here with me, so use one of the employees to handle the carriage, one of the security people perhaps. They never seem to do anything, anyway, and one or two of them can certainly be spared.'

'Yes, ma'am.'

'You will consider yourselves to be under his instruction. Is that clear, Toby?'

'Yes, ma'am.'

'Good. Captain, I want you to approach bankers in Denver. You already know where we do our business, but you needn't limit yourself to that bank. Look for the best terms you can get on a loan. Explain your ideas for recovery and seek whatever amount you feel is needed. You can send word back when you have some suitable candidates, and Kenneth will join you at that time to sign whatever agreements you've reached with the bank. You can pledge shares in the Irish Rover as collateral, if necessary. Up to but not exceeding forty nine percent. Is that clear, Captain?'

'Quite clear.'

'Toby?'

'Yes, Miss Beth. Completely clear.'

'Good.' Her smile, one of the sincere ones, flickered again, directed first to Toby Madison and then to Alex. 'Thank you. Both of you. Now, get on with your work, please. The quicker this is done, the better.'

Madison led their way back to the foyer and into the vestibule where the cold lay waiting.

XIV

The weather that had been moving in wasn't moving in any longer. It was there. And it was extreme. High, biting wind, bone-chilling temperatures, and snow whipping parallel to the ground made Alex glad they were inside the protection of the closed carriage.

There was no heat inside, but at least the flimsy walls and isinglass side curtains kept most of the wind out. He felt sorry for the two men who were riding up on the driving box, both of them bundled deep into heavy garments, gloves, and scarves, so that all which could be seen of them were their eyes. Even their noses were covered with heavy, knitted mufflers. A loose rime of ice developed over their noses and mouths where the moisture from their breath came through.

Alex hadn't seen weather like this since the last time he'd had to transit the far north of the Atlantic. And that had not been by choice. He'd spotted the sails of a Union corsair, one of those that stood off the English ports in an effort to catch Confederate blockade runners while they were heavily loaded and the crews still half drunk from liberty in a peacetime port. The privately owned ships preyed upon the Confederacy with the blessings of their country, killing and robbing the brave rebels of their cargoes.

On this occasion, Alex was not sure if the damn Yankee devil saw him as well, but took no chances, diverting his course far to the north of the normal lanes. The *Belle* had cannon mounted, but risking crew and cargo was never his inclination. He much preferred running to battle. And so he did that time as well when he drove his ship into the belly of a storm. The northern Atlantic weather had been terrible. Although hardly a nuisance as compared with the cannon of a corsair.

Bad as it was, though, it was no worse than this mountain storm. The blessing was that here there were no mountainous waves to threaten ship and crew. The road they followed remained steady under the wheels of the carriage, and if Alex could not see where they were going, it was of no consequence. The drivers and the horses were responsible for that.

All he had to do was sit there trying to mentally create a genuine business reorganization plan from the truly rather vague impressions he'd conveyed to Kenneth O'Reilly.

He huddled inside the upturned

collar of his coat and tried to work out how best to approach the bank officers in Denver.

XV

'Sorry, gents, sorry, dammit. One of the horses is limping on his nigh forefoot. Got to lay over until we see what's wrong. Sorry.'

They were stopped in . . . Alex had no earthly idea where they were stopped. Somewhere between Holihan and Denver. That much was obvious. That much was all he could deduce.

One of the drivers swung the door open, admitting a blast of arctic air and grainy snow that stung like birdshot on Alex's cheeks. He ducked even deeper inside his coat, wishing he'd brought a muffler to swaddle his head like the drivers did.

Toby Madison climbed out, and Alex quickly followed.

'This way,' The driver — or his

assistant, Alex could not tell one from the other even by their coats, because now their garments were all caked solid white with clinging snow — led them at a shuffling run, all four men bent over in an effort to cope with the wind. They reached a dark, gaping hole in the face of a low cliff, and the guide dashed inside.

Alex still did not know where they were, but it was obvious the hole was man-made, not naturally occurring. He could see tool marks on the walls and ceiling. It was, he guessed, either an abandoned mine or the prospect hole where someone once hoped there would be a mine.

The driver lighted a bull's-eye lantern and shined the light into the tunnel to help them along.

Except it wasn't a tunnel at all, Alex remembered. Or anyway, he assumed it was not. A tunnel is something that runs completely through an obstruction with openings at both ends. A hole bored into a mountain but not carried all the way through — it took him a moment to recall the word he'd first encountered in the Irish Rover books and had to turn to John Barkley for explanation — that was an adit. A hole dug downward is a shaft. And a hole dug upward is a stope. So this was very likely an adit. Alex felt a momentary pride that he should know these things now that he was associated with the mining industry.

'Here,' the man with the lantern said.

They were deep enough inside the ground that the terrible cold outside could not penetrate. Quite. It was chilly here but not so harshly, bitterly cold as it was outdoors. 'This oughta be as good a place as any.'

'Fine,' Madison agreed. 'Just be careful you don't take it too far. Not till we know what we need to find out.'

Alex had no idea what they were talking about.

The two drivers stripped off their mittens and unwrapped the ice-brittle mufflers from around their heads.

And Alex's gut turned colder than the winter storm could have made him.

The look of these men, seeing them now . . . he remembered.

These were the two men who'd beaten and robbed him in Rattlesnake Hollow.

7

I

They grabbed hold of his upper arms, Madison on his left and the smaller of the two thugs on his right. The third one, the biggest of them, very carefully unbuttoned Alex's coat. That one pulled Alex's hat off and tossed it aside. Then, with the cooperation of his pals, he removed the coat as well.

'You sons of bitches.'

They ignored him.

It took no particular genius for him to figure out why they wanted the heavy buffalo-hide coat off. The thick, curly shag would absorb much of the force from a punch. And these men had every intention of inflicting pain. Much pain.

At least, Alex thought, that cruel SOB Dan Tyler hadn't come along. Alex had seen what he did to the inept robber back in Holihan.

The tall one threw Alex's coat to the floor near his hat, and the man who was holding Alex's right arm yelped. 'Careful, dammit, you're gonna get it dirty. That's a nice coat, Gary. I want it, so just hold on there for a minute.' He let go of Alex's arm and snatched the coat off the stone floor, brushing it to remove any dirt that might have gotten onto it, then hung it on a spike that protruded from one of the wooden shoring timbers that lined both side walls and lay across the ceiling every five or six feet.

'Can I proceed now, Hank?'

'Go ahead. Have fun.'

The one called Gary grinned. He pulled Alex's shirt open and looked at his torso for a moment as if assessing it.

And then, with deliberate force and careful placement, he broke the bottommost of Alex's left ribs.

II

Dan Tyler probably took lessons from this plug-ugly named Gary. The man did know how to inflict pain. No doubt that could be considered a talent. If so, it was one for which Alex had no appreciation whatsoever.

'Adamley. Alex. Listen to me.'

Alex ignored him.

'Please, Alex,' Toby Madison tried again. 'I like you, Alex. I don't want to see you hurt like this. Just give me the paper Miss Beth wants from you. Tell me where it is. They'll stop as soon as they know where your paper is. Please, Alex. Don't make me have them keep doing this to you. Tell me, Alex. I'll make them stop. I promise you. I'll make them stop.'

Alex could still see out of his right eye. Madison was on his left side, so he had to turn his head far to that side in order to see the man. He gave Madison what he hoped was a withering glare, then took careful aim and spat in the man's face.

Gary hit him again. Not so judiciously this time but in anger. The force of that untrammeled blow exploded inside Alex like a cannon shot and drove the air from him. His knees buckled, and he nearly slipped from the grasp of the two who were holding him.

Alex took that as an opportunity and let himself go limp between them, feigning unconsciousness.

They stretched him out onto the cold stone flooring and tried to revive him, but Alex kept his eyes closed, his mouth sagging open, and his breathing shallow.

'Wake up, Alex. You got to wake up and tell me. We'll leave you be then. Please, Alex.'

'Ah, the sonuvabitch is out cold, Toby. And I'm freezing cold, too.' Alex heard Gary laugh. 'It ain't so bad for you, but I been working up a sweat. Listen, it could be two, three hours before he wakes up. Tell you what, let's go down to the cabin and get a fire going. We'll warm up a little, then come back when he's awake.'

Alex hoped they would just walk away and leave him there, but he had no such luck. They rolled him over and pulled his arms behind him, probably so they could tie his hands together.

Except he had no right wrist to get a wrap on. They settled for tying a rope onto his left wrist and dragging him to the side of the tunnel — adit, dammit — and tying the rope onto something else.

'That should hold him,' Gary said. 'An' don't you worry none. When we get back, he'll tell you everything he's ever known. Believe me.'

Alex heard footsteps recede toward the mouth of the adit.

Gary was wrong, of course.

No matter what that animal did to him, Alex was not going to tell them where the deed was. As soon as he did that, he would be a dead man. There was no way they would allow him to leave this cave.

And, dammit, even if he got to the point of thinking death would be a relief and a joy, just to make the hurting stop, he still would not tell them where the damned deed was, if only to piss them off.

They might kill him. Very likely they would. But he'd be damned if he would let them break him, too.

III

Alex sat up, wincing but alert, and surveyed his situation. The rope on his wrist was tied in a neat square knot. It was a landlubber's knot of absolutely no use to a sailor. But it was quick, it was easy, it was strong, and pretty much everyone knew how to tie one. Alex was pleased to see this one. As easy as a square knot is to tie, they are just as easy to untie.

He lifted his hand and bit delicately into the fibers of the knot, tugging with his teeth this way and that.

Gently. A little on this side. A little on that.

All he would need would be a few minutes of patience and close attention. He expected he could manage that.

IV

Hank, bless him, hadn't yet decided to take possession of 'his' new buffalo coat. It still dangled from the spike where he'd hung it. Alex thought he would break in two from the agony of standing up and walking over there.

But there was no question about what needed to be done. He stood upright, regardless of the pain that it caused him — less, however, than if he stayed and waited for Toby Madison and friends to return — and he walked over there to retrieve his coat and his hat.

He pulled the coat on and, before anything else, felt the inside breast pocket.

The lump, hard but not too heavy, was still there.

He hadn't had a chance yet to practice with the little breaktop Smith and Wesson revolver. Hadn't thought to bring any more of the self-contained cartridges with him. That was all right. He had the means to defend himself. He had five of the little cartridges in the cylinder of the revolver.

Best of all, he had the element of surprise. None of the men knew Alex was armed.

Alex transferred the gun into the left-hand side pocket on the coat for easier access, then buttoned the coat and turned the collar high.

He was bent double with pain and leaned on the adit wall for support. But he was able to move.

He made his way out of the lantern light and on toward the storm he could hear still roaring through the canyon.

V

A sensible man would head immediately for Denver City. Or, if he had any faith in whatever local law might be available to an itinerant stranger, he would rush to the country seat in search of a judge capable of swearing out warrants and a sheriff able to serve them.

That was what a sensible man would do. It was also what Madison and company would almost certainly expect.

Avoiding the expected was one solid reason why Alex should turn back into the teeth of the wind.

Anger was an equally good reason.

Alex's enemies were back there in Holihan. And while he might not know where he was just now, he damn sure knew which way the wind had been blowing the entire time they'd been riding in that carriage. No seaman was ever unaware of something so basic as that. The wind had come from behind ever since they left the O'Reilly house back in town. In order to return, all

Alex had to do was put his nose into the wind and walk.

He considered trying to find the team so he could steal a horse to make the journey easier. He quickly rejected the thought. He doubted he could force a horse to face this wind, even if he had two good hands to work with. And he quite frankly did not want to risk spending any more time than was absolutely necessary in the same vicinity where Gary and Hank and Toby Madison were.

Just as when he'd had to travel in the teeth of danger from damn Yankee warships and privateering corsairs, he would much rather avoid confrontation if possible. Cannon or pistol, there were better means of defense. And being out of the enemy's reach was his favorite of them all.

Alex covered his face as completely as he could and began walking into the blowing snow.

VI

Maybe he should have stayed back there in the abandoned mine. He could have grabbed his coat and hat and sneaked deeper inside the adit instead of coming out here into the teeth of the worst damned storm he could ever remember enduring. Far and away the worst he'd ever seen on land, anyway.

Madison and friends almost certainly would have found him missing, assumed he went outside, and run after him.

Almost certainly. That was not guaranteed.

And anyway, it was much too late now to change his mind. He'd been gone . . . what? . . . an hour or longer? He truly was not sure how much time had passed. A man's perception becomes skewed during periods of stress and danger anyway, and today his body, mind, and emotions were under assault from all points of the compass simultaneously. He was guessing an hour. It could have been several. Or it could have been ten minutes. He had no way to judge.

It was certain, though, that he would not turn around now. Hell, if he did turn back, he was not sure he would even be able to find the mine opening. Visibility was down to a half dozen feet or so. Not only was snow continuing to fall, but previously fallen snow was being picked up and carried on the wind, too.

The ground beneath his feet was completely bare for the most part. That was to the good. What was not so good was that where it was not bare, where the snow was caught by some obstruction and spilled out of the wind, deep drifts were quickly built.

Alex pushed through several that were chest deep. The drifts were made all the worse because the snow had not yet had time to compact itself or to form a crust, so instead of supporting his weight, it remained loose and had to be breasted with brute force. Pushing through the deeper drifts was as difficult and as slow as if he were wading through cold molasses.

He could not see well enough to follow the road that lay between the mine and Holihan, so all he could do was to keep his face in the wind and walk doggedly forward.

He long since lost all sensation in his nose, cheeks, and ears, and the only thing he could feel in his lips was the sting where they were dry and cracked. He tried once to wipe his mouth but came away with flecks of red ice on the back of his glove. Blood that had frozen solid onto his flesh.

And that was probably a good thing because the ice, whether formed of blood or spittle, would act as a barrier to further damage and actually hold body heat beneath the frigid coating. Alex had seen that often enough at sea and expected it to work no differently here.

In very much that same way, most of his face was protected by the crust of snow that stuck to his beard and mustache. Body heat melted the snow, and it immediately froze into a sheet of ice, rigid armor that kept the wind out amazingly well. Alex felt it with the back of his hand — he was losing feeling in his fingertips and did not trust them to relay a true picture of what they touched — but was careful to avoid breaking this hoary crust.

He gave his concentration to small details such as these. And while he did so, he continued pressing forward, asking his battered, aching body for only one step forward. One step. One step. One step more. Over and over and over again.

He walked blindly, closing his eyes most of the time and accepting the wind as his guide. It hurt to open his eyes to the wind, and he opened them briefly and seldom to look ahead.

Alex had no idea how long he walked or how far.

He only knew that he had to keep on walking. Had to keep Madison and Gary and Hank from catching up with him.

Had to avoid those sons of bitches, not merely to flee from them. He also wanted to best them.

Them and the treacherous bitch who'd sent them.

And so he walked. Steadily. Doggedly. Without thought or rest. His concentration was total. Forward. One step. One step. One step.

VII

He could go no farther.

For long moments he stood there. Brutishly numb. Unaware of everything except for the fact that his progress was halted, except for the fact that his way was blocked.

It took him time to work out why.

Something was in his way. He had walked into something tall, wide, and solid. He stood for a time facing it. Blinking. Trying to work out what this thing was that he walked into.

He was cold. But less so. It was the

wind, he finally and after much thought determined. The wind stopped. Except it hadn't stopped. He could still hear it whine and whistle. But he no longer felt it.

For quite some time, he hadn't felt the cut of the wind. But he had been conscious of the force of it. He'd had to lean into it in order to keep his balance and avoid being blown backward. He'd had to bend forward at the waist and push his way into the wind. Now that strong presence was missing. He felt no thrust of wind at all.

Ah! Of course. Whatever this thing was that stood in front of him, it blocked the wind from reaching him. Silly of him to take so long to think through such a simple thing as that. Alex felt foolish. So foolish and inept and useless that he began to cry. Tears froze on his cheeks and in his beard. He could sense the damp warmth for only a moment and then felt the tiny nuggets of ice on his skin. Those were the first sensations he could remember feeling on any exposed part of him practically since he started out. And that had been . . . God only knew how long ago. Hours? He did not know.

He knew only that he needed to move on. He could no longer remember why he needed to move or where he needed to go, but he was sure that he quite desperately needed to continue forward.

The wall in front of him stopped him from doing that. The wall —

Wall? He blinked. Stared. Yes. Wall.

He recognized that now. Thick, split-log boards were laid up in horizontal rows to form a wall. He'd walked blindly into somebody's wall. That was laughable, wasn't it? He did not feel like laughing.

A building. Town? Had he reached the town? Perhaps so. He wasn't sure. Perhaps he could walk around the wall and see what he found there.

That would take him back out into the wind. He could hear the wind howl in frustration at its inability to reach him, to freeze him, to destroy him. The wind was not going to do that. He would not permit it. Wouldn't give in to those men, either. He would walk around the wall and look.

He did. He turned to his left. Walked close beside the wall. Into the cut of the wind. Leaned into it again. Saw lights. Lamplight. Somehow it had grown dark, or nearly so, since he set out into the cold and the wind and the snow. He hadn't noticed at the time.

But now there were lights.

The lights drew him to them as a moth is drawn to flame.

He stood outside, peering in through the window, trying to remember how he should go about going in where the light was. Where warmth was.

He could not remember.

He stood there. Mute. Motionless. Not even shivering any longer. He felt, in fact, quite comfortably detached from the unpleasantness of his body.

Alex felt as if he were floating. Serene

288

and unconcerned. Really quite happy.

He heard something, a thump, and for a brief instant, the wind that pressed against his shoulder lessened. Then he heard a cry.

'Jesus Christ, Eddie! There's a dead man out here. Come help me bring him in and see who he is.'

VIII

'Geez, Jimmy, no. Don't put him so close to the stove. We warm him up too quick, and he could damn die.'

'He's already dead.'

'No, he isn't. Look there.'

'He sure looked dead.'

'Well, he isn't. Now help me drag him over into the corner. We'll lay him on that table where we can get to him. Ira! Grab that basin behind the bar and run outside for a minute. I need you to fill it with snow.'

'What the hell d'you want snow for, Eddie?'

'Got to rub his face with snow. Keep him from warming too fast. Don't argue with me now, Ira. Just do it. Please. Then you can draw yourself a free beer. But not till you bring that basin of snow. And full, mind. We'll be needing plenty.

'Ok, that's good. Open his coat, Jimmy. We'll let some warmth reach him. Not too much and not too fast, but we got to get him warm again. And his boots. Pull off his boots. Socks, too, if he's wearing any. We need to see are his feet as bad off as his face is.

'Thanks. You see how I'm rubbing his cheeks and face and all? I want you to keep rubbing the snow on him just like that. You see how pale and waxy the skin looks right here? I want you to rub the snow everyplace his skin is all white and pale like that.'

'Where're you going, Eddie?'

'I got to fetch a kettle and heat some water. No, I think I'll heat some of that apple cider Burl brought up from Denver last trip. We need to see if we can get something warm into his belly. The cider oughta be just about right. It'll be hot and nourishing, too. You go ahead now, Ira. Jimmy, you help him. One of you gets tired of rubbing, the other take over. And keep the snow coming. Don't let that basin get empty. Whoever isn't rubbing can fill the basin again when it's needed. You hear? Keep going there. I'll be back with that hot cider quick as I can.'

IX

His face was on fire. Alex felt like the flesh was burning off his whole face. The sensation was that of pins and needles, like when your foot goes to sleep and the circulation suddenly returns, except this was carried to an extreme that was agony.

He screamed, and strong hands held him down.

Someone touched his cheek, and the pain was so awful he screamed again.

He could not help himself.

His feet tingled and burned, too, but not nearly so bad as his face.

On his cheeks, his forehead, even under his beard, he felt the return of blood to the surface from which it had been driven by the cold.

Alex opened his eyes. He recognized one of the men who were crowded close around him. The fellow was one of the bartenders at a saloon in Holihan. Alex did not know the man's name, but he recognized him. The others — and there must have been a dozen or more — were all complete strangers.

'The hurting will last a while, mister, but it will stop,' the bartender said. 'The ends of your earlobes are black. So is part of one nostril. Those will fall off. They won't grow back. But they won't look so terrible bad, and the good news is that you're gonna live. You damn near didn't. How'd you come to be out in this weather, anyway? Did you get lost coming down off the hill or something?'

Alex shook his head. He very nearly blurted out exactly what it was that did happen to him.

But he stopped himself in time to keep from saying anything.

He was in no shape right now to confront anyone. Especially anyone like Toby Madison or Gary or the third one — it took him a moment to remember that one's name — Hank.

Not even Beth O'Reilly.

He just was in no shape to do much of anything right now except writhe in pain while his body warmed and tried to return itself to normal.

'Help me . . . sit up . . . please.'

Willing hands grasped him under his shoulders and lifted him into a sitting position. He was perched on the edge of a table that threatened to overturn, so they picked him up and set him onto a chair instead. He could see his boots and coat on a nearby table.

The revolver was in the pocket of his coat, and a moment of panic threatened to overwhelm him when he realized that if Madison and those others walked in right now, he would be unable to defend himself.

He had to get out of here. Quickly, before they caught up with him. He had no idea how long it was since he left the mine, but even if they searched for him in the wrong direction, they would soon enough think to look toward Holihan, too.

And Alex was in no condition to resist them. Not at this moment.

He needed somewhere to hide while he got some strength back. And while he worked out what he should do now.

He was *not* going to turn and run though. Not this time.

They'd done too much. He'd absorbed too much. He intended to take no more.

Now it was his intention to turn and face whatever shot and shell came his way.

Damn them anyway.

'Hand me . . . my boots . . . please.'

Someone did, and Alex stuffed his feet into them. Even that hurt.

With an effort, he got to his feet. His face still burned, and he was weak and shaking. He felt as spineless as a straw-stuffed scarecrow. Physically. *Only* in the physical sense.

He reached for his coat.

'Mister, you can't go outside again. You aren't up to it.'

Alex smiled at him. 'Got to. But I'll be back. I promise you, friend. I will be back.'

He already knew exactly where he intended to go so he could finish the job of warming himself and resting.

He knew where, and he had to get there before Toby Madison returned to Holihan to finish the job he'd started.

Alex pulled the heavy coat on. He could not manage the buttons. His fingers did not work that well at the moment. That was all right. Even hanging loose, it would offer enough protection.

Alex thanked the men whose kindness had kept him alive, mentally setting down the face of each so someday if ever he could, he would repay them as best he might be able.

Then, still so weak he staggered and swayed, he walked outside again into the gale and the blowing snow.

X

Both men jumped nearly out of their skins when Marc Anthony Jones returned to his cabin late that evening, Jones because he walked in to find a most unexpected visitor inside his place and Alex because he'd dropped off to sleep while waiting for the only friend he had in Holihan. When the door opened and a chill breeze swept into the cabin, Alex woke, thinking Madison had come for him.

'Alex! What . . . you look terrible. What's happened?' Alex told him. Part of it, anyway.

'Why ever would they do such a thing, Alex?'

'I have something they want.'

'Want rather badly, I would say,' Jones said.

'Bad enough to commit murder.'

Marc came across the room to the crude chair where Alex was sitting and bent down to examine him closely. 'You will heal, Alex. But you will never look exactly the same as you did this morning.'

Alex scowled. But there was no help for it now. And he'd lost more than just his looks before this day. He supposed he should be grateful to still be alive.

'You can hide here as long as you need to, Alex,' Jones told him. 'Then we'll spirit you out at night so they can't find you again.'

Alex chuckled. 'Marc, my friend, I didn't come back here to hide. I came back here to fight them.'

'Be realistic, Alex. You are one man. And, if I may mention it, perhaps not at your best. They are many. The entire security force from the Irish Rover will follow whatever Toby Madison and Dan Tyler tell them to do. They are hard men, Alex, and they would come for you all at once. They would — '

'Not that kind of fight, Marc. I don't intend that sort of fight at all,' Alex interrupted.

Jones gave him a puzzled look. 'What do you mean then?'

Alex grinned — there was not a hint of mirth in that expression, however — and told him.

8

I

Alex waited three days before he engaged his enemy. The delay was not so much to give time for Madison and the others to return to Holihan, not so much to make sure the O'Reillys would know by now that they had not succeeded in wresting the deed from this one-armed fugitive from the sea. It was really because it took that long for Alex to recover his strength enough that he thought he could walk down the hill from Marc Anthony Jones's cabin without collapsing. And even after three days, he was pressing himself.

Still, he wanted it done. And done quickly. The longer he waited, the more likely it was that someone would remember that he'd been seen in Jones's company on more than one occasion. It would take the speculation of only one man in order for them to come here to find him, and his plan required that he be the one to initiate hostilities. So just before dawn on a frigid Sunday morning, Alex stepped out into the crisp, still air and made his way downhill through a landscape that was starkly streaked black and white by the darkness hiding stone and the pale lines drawn by snow drifted deep in the recent storm.

He still carried the little revolver in his left-hand coat pocket, but he had no ammunition for it other than the five cartridges it already held. He naturally had not been able to return to his own cabin for the boxes of spare ammunition he'd bought earlier, and if Marc purchased the rare, self-contained cartridges for him, the act would have attracted instant attention.

Besides, with a fair wind and smooth seas, he would not need a firearm to resolve this particular fight.

Alex slipped into town before most

folk were awake. He made his way along the bank of the creek, keeping out of sight behind the commercial buildings and very few residences on that side of the street, and entered the outhouse behind the saloon where he'd been so kindly received just a few days earlier. He did not remember the name of the place, but Marc knew immediately when Alex told him who the bartender was.

'That's Eddie Wainwright. Good man,' Marc said.

'A good man indeed, bless him.' Eddie, Alex thought. So the voices he'd heard were not a dream after all. He hadn't really been sure until this moment that the conversation he overheard that night was real. Apparently it was. He must not have been completely unconscious at the time.

Alex felt his way inside the one-hole outhouse. He carefully latched the door against unwanted intrusion, then perched on the edge of the seat. Even as cold as it was, the outhouse had a dank and heavy stink. He guessed the contents were deep enough in the earth that they hadn't frozen.

Up above, however, the tiny building was plenty cold. Alex was in for an uncomfortable wait.

That was all right. He'd been more uncomfortable than this a time or two in the past. At least this discomfort was undertaken for good cause.

He sat patiently while the sun came up, while the sounds of the town waking came to him through the flimsy wooden sides of the outhouse, while three times, someone rattled the door, trying to get in.

'Sorry,' he said in a deliberately husky voice. 'Got the runs. You better go someplace else.'

He waited until he heard a soft tapping on the side wall and Marc's voice telling him, 'All right, Alex. Five minutes.'

'I'll be there.'

II

He was nervous. It helped, at least a little, to stick his hand inside the coat pocket and feel the cold steel of the Smith and Wesson. He was not counting on the gun, but he was almighty glad it was there.

At the end of five minutes — more or less — he unlatched the outhouse door and walked across the trash-strewn backyard and into the saloon.

There was the usual Sunday-morning crowd there. Plus those extra invited guests brought in by express invitation as delivered early in the morning by Marc Jones.

Neither Madison nor Tyler noticed Alex's arrival through the back door, but they certainly saw him when he hopped up onto the chair conveniently set in place by Marc and onto the bar top.

As soon as Alex was standing on the bar, towering above the heads of all present, Marc rattled a cow bell to call everyone's attention. Other noisemakers might have been more appropriate, but the cow bell was all Marc could find short of firing a gun indoors and starting a panic. And emptying the place was not at all what Alex had in mind here.

'Gentlemen. Gentlemen. Listen to me. Some of you remember me from the Irish Rover. Some of you I've seen in the saloons and gaming rooms. And I am sure a few of you will remember me from a few nights ago when I turned up here more frozen than alive.'

He pointed to his face. 'You see these bruises. I want to tell you how I got them. I want to tell you — '

'Don't let the lying little son of a bitch say another word,' Tyler roared. Toby Madison, Alex saw, was busy sneaking out the front while Tyler occupied the attention of the crowd. Gone to tell his master and mistress, the O'Reillys, what was happening here, Alex guessed.

'He was fired from the Rover,' Tyler

shouted. 'He said he was gonna get even. This must be what he meant.'

'Hear me out,' Alex responded. 'Then I will leave it to you good people of Holihan to judge who is lying and who is telling the truth of it.'

He had the full attention of the crowd now. Oh my, but he most certainly did.

Carefully, sharply cutting Tyler off each time the man tried to interrupt, Alex began telling this crowd of honest miners what he underwent since he got here.

They listened. But he could tell all too soon that his audience was skeptical.

Tyler had a response for every comment Alex made, the security chief's answer usually having to do with Alex's supposed firing from the Irish Rover and the threats Tyler claimed he made when he was forced out of the office.

'He's made this up,' Tyler shouted. 'You know the O'Reillys. Hell, they've given you your jobs. You owe everything you have to Ken O'Reilly. Now, who are you gonna listen to? Ken O'Reilly? Or this cripple from God knows where? Damned rebel is what I'd say he is. Listen to that accent. Son of a bitch got a mouth full of honey an' cotton. Ken and the rest of us supported the Union, boys. Are you gonna let some grayback son of a bitch come along now and lie about a patriot?'

'He's right, mister. We don't know you from Adam's off ox. Where the hell do you come from? And why would somebody like Ken O'Reilly be after you, anyhow? You don't look like you got much more'n what you're wearing on your back.'

'What I have is a deed to a mining claim,' Alex shot back at whoever the man was who'd spoken. 'O'Reilly's lousy business practices have just about busted the Rover. I guess he thought if he could steal my deed, he'd be able to get back on top somehow.'

'Fine. Show us this deed,' someone yelled.

'Show us.'

'You made the claim. Now prove up on it, Johnny Reb,' another voice cried.

'I don't . . . I don't have it on me,' Alex said. The response sounded lame, even to him.

'Then what proof do you have?' one of the miners demanded.

'I don't. I've been beat on. Robbed. Left for dead once and damn near died of exposure a second time. Dammit, they even stole my dog.'

For some reason, the accusation about the dog brought from this crowd a murmur of sympathy that hadn't been present when he told them about the beatings and the robbery.

Dan Tyler looked like a nerve ending had been struck, and someone loudly asked, 'I remember that dog you got recent, Tyler. Where'd you say you got him? And you, mister. What'd this dog of yours look like?'

'I didn't say, but the fact is, it's only a

pup. He was taken from me about a month and a half ago. Ordinary little Indian-bred mongrel, he was. Brown. Floppy ears. Sort of a ratty tail.'

'I remember that pup when you were first in my store, Adamley. The little fella piddled on my floor. Sure I remember him.'

'That damn sure sounds like your dog, Tyler. You want to tell us about this?'

Just that quickly, the mood of the crowd swung 180 degrees around, aimed not at Alex any longer but with the finger of angry accusation pointed squarely at Dan Tyler now.

'I've seen your dog, Tyler. So tell us. How would this fella know what your dog looks like when he's never seen the pup?'

'I say he never had no damned dog,' Tyler bawled. Then he clamped his jaw hard shut and turned pale. The storekeeper already said he remembered the pup, even remembered it peeing on his floor.

Skepticism turned to fury, and Dan Tyler turned and ran for the door in order to escape before someone threw a punch and launched a melee that would find him on the receiving end of a mob's attentions.

A dozen men boiled out of the saloon in pursuit of him.

Alex looked down at Marc Anthony Jones. He smiled. 'I think they believe me now, Marc. I do believe they do.'

Jones held his hand up to steady Alex and help him down to floor level.

III

'May I speak with you for a moment?'

'Certainly. I'll be glad to hear you out,' Alex said politely, 'but I'd like to go find my dog now, if you don't mind.'

'Please. Just for a minute?' The gentleman's request was politely posed but insistent. 'It's important.'

Alex looked at him. Whoever this man was, he did not look like much. He wore corduroy trousers and engineer's boots laced to the knee, a red-and-black-checked flannel shirt, and a pair of disreputable galluses that looked like they should have been granted honorable retirement years ago.

Still, he had something to say, and it was important, at least to him.

'All right.'

The man smiled, glanced once at Alex's empty right sleeve, and extended his left hand to shake. Alex was taken aback. But not so much so that he failed to accept the handshake. It felt . . . unusual. But he liked it. Considering.

'Where are you from, sir?' the man asked.

'Georgia.'

The smile became larger. 'I thought so. It's an accent I've heard before.'

'You are not Southern yourself,' Alex said.

'No. I'm from Canada. You can consider me neutral, if it matters.'

Alex shook his head. 'No, sir, I guess

it doesn't. Not any longer.'

'Good. That is a healthy attitude. You mentioned a little while ago that you own a deed. Would you mind telling me what this deed covers?'

'I . . . don't know that that would be a good idea. A gentleman once told me that Henry Holihan might want me dead if he finds out about it. Which I suppose he must learn soon. And Lord knows, the O'Reillys were desperate enough to kill to get it. I suppose it shouldn't surprise me if Holihan feels the same way.'

The gentleman threw his head back and roared with laughter.

'That may well be amusing to you, sir, but that's an opinion I fail to share. Forgive me for that, please, but — '

'No, no.' The man wiped his eyes and grinned. 'You misunderstand me. It is not your death that I find laughable but the accusation that was made by someone who surely knew better.'

'And how is that, sir?'

'Mr Adamley, I am Henry Holihan.

And I can assure you, sir, that I have no designs upon your life. Quite the contrary. If yours is the deed to Number Eight, you are the owner of twenty percent of the Big H. You would be, in fact, my partner in the venture.'

'P-pardon me?'

'The Big H consists of five claims. I own three of them outright and leased the fourth from a gentleman who didn't like the winters here and removed himself to Santa Fe. The fifth claim was owned by a group of Georgians. After the Big H proved out, I tried to find them, but they'd all disappeared into the war. I, uh, don't suppose you could tell me about them?'

If this was a test of a sort, it was one Alex would likely fail. 'I never knew them, Mr Holihan. My brother made them a loan so they could join the gold rush here in fifty-eight. When war broke out, they returned home. They had no money, but they wanted to outfit themselves this time to join the cavalry. My brother gave them cash again, and they signed over the deed in his favor. My brother did not survive the war, and I inherited the deed. I have no idea what happened to the young gentlemen who came here in search of their fortune.'

'I see. And you say you do have the deed?'

'I have it put safely away. I can produce it when necessary.'

'Fine,' Holihan said. 'If you can do that, you will find that since the outset, I set up a separate account in favor of whoever owns that one-fifth share. I put a fifth of all profits into it and withdrew a share of all capital expenses. Does that sound fair, Mr Adamley?'

'More than fair, Mr Holihan.'

'Good. Because if you can show me that deed, you are going to find yourself in possession of a very tidy sum of money plus an ongoing share in the Big H for however long it may last.'

'What about . . . ?' He inclined his head in the direction of the canyon wall where the Irish Rover lay.

'Mining men are for the most part very fair, Mr Adamley. I believe you will find this to be true. But they are not forgiving. I suspect by now Toby Madison and that unpleasant thug Tyler and all their men have started running for their lives. They will not likely return. As for the O'Reillys . . . if I were you, Mr Adamley, I would not count too much on the likelihood of either one of them ever being charged with a crime. Not without hard evidence or at the very least the testimony of Madison and Tyler.'

'I'm sure you are right, Mr Holihan.'

'I hope you won't attempt to take the issue into your own hands . . . ' His smile flashed again. 'Excuse me . . . hand.'

Alex laughed. He liked this Holihan fellow. Damned if he didn't. 'No, sir, I believe you will find that I'm a very mild and inoffensive soul. I bend with the wind and cause no man trouble.'

Holihan looked at him.

And laughed. Loudly.

We do hope that you have enjoyed reading this large print book.

Did you know that all of our titles are available for purchase?

We publish a wide range of high quality large print books including:
Romances, Mysteries, Classics
General Fiction
Non Fiction and Westerns

Special interest titles available in large print are:
The Little Oxford Dictionary
Music Book, Song Book
Hymn Book, Service Book

Also available from us courtesy of Oxford University Press:
Young Readers' Dictionary
(large print edition)
Young Readers' Thesaurus
(large print edition)

For further information or a free brochure, please contact us at:
Ulverscroft Large Print Books Ltd.,
The Green, Bradgate Road, Anstey,
Leicester, LE7 7FU, England.
Tel: (00 44) **0116 236 4325**
Fax: (00 44) **0116 234 0205**

Other titles in the
Linford Western Library:

WARRICK'S BATTLE

Terrell L. Bowers

Haunted by the past, Paul Warrick is assailed by bad memories, and in an attempt to forget, drifts from town to town finding work. But a shoot-out at a casino lands him in jail, and with the valley on the verge of a range war, Paul's actions might be the fire to light the fuse. Paul becomes involved in the final show-down — and he must not only save his life, but also his own sanity at the same time!

MAN OF BLOOD

Lee Lejeune

When he visits his brother, Texas Ranger Tom Flint finds Hank dying and his wife Abby abducted after an attack on their homestead. Soon Flint runs up against a gang of vicious layabouts working for Rodney Ravenshaw, who is trying to retrieve family property by underhand means. Can Flint live up to his Comanche name of Man of Blood and save his brother's homestead by ridding the town of Willow Creek of its nest of vipers?

TROUBLE AT BRODIE CREEK

Ben Coady

Sam Hanley, marshal of Brodie Creek, has resigned to marry and become a rancher. However, trouble hits town when the Thad Cross gang — all killers — arrive. To avert disaster the townsfolk want Hanley back as marshal, but Hanley only becomes involved when the Cross gang raid the bank and kidnap his new wife, Ellie. To rescue Ellie he must follow Cross to Hangman's Perch, an impregnable outlaw roost. Everything seems stacked against him — can Hanley win through?

WHERE ONE MAN STANDS

Chad Hammer

The brothers had never been close —until a killer cut down their father at the end of the long trail drive. That was the day their world would change forever. Side by side they set out to battle the killer they hunted and the murderous desert. Until that day and hour when they faced their man, not as enemies but as true brothers with but a single thought. Revenge or death! They would accept nothing less — together.

SIDEWINDER FLATS

Walt Masterton

When horse trader Con Carnigan's cavalry horses are stolen, he faces starvation if he cannot retrieve them. He tracks them to Sidewinder Flats in the Sonoran Desert, but finds himself in the domain of a western Fagin. The town is a robbers' roost run by Hoffman, who offers Carnigan the sheriff's job, so long as he turns a blind eye to the criminals. Carnigan however, takes the job seriously, as Hoffman and his cohorts discover . . .